The Dark Horse

Rumer Godden
The Dark Horse

The Viking Press *New York*

Copyright © 1981 by Rumer Godden

First published in 1982 by The Viking Press
625 Madison Avenue, New York, N.Y. 10022

Library of Congress Cataloging in Publication Data
Godden, Rumer, 1907–
The dark horse.
I. Title.
PR6013.02D3   1982   823′.912   81-10352
ISBN 0-670-25664-1   AACR2

This book appeared originally in different form
as a *Reader's Digest Condensed Book.*

Printed in the United States of America

This novel is based on
a version by
Sir Owain Jenkins
and aided and abetted by him

Author's Note

This story is taken from an event that happened in Calcutta some fifty years ago and has become a legend in Calcutta's racing circles. It has been published several times in different versions with a variety of characters, but always as an anecdote among other anecdotes. It is documented in the official history of The Royal Calcutta Turf Club, but I have called the Sisters concerned The Sisters of Poverty, because the real Order in the story prefers to remain hidden.

The Dark Horse

Prologue

He was born in Ireland in the early thirties, a big foal even longer-legged than usual, legs that were slender but strong, already showing incipient power. His eyes, as with all foals, looked over-large in his narrow fine-boned face; his nostrils were large too. At birth he was black with the usual lighter ridge of mane and pampas flock of tail. His dam was Black Tulip, he was sired by Bold Crusader and so was registered as Dark Invader but, for two days of his life, he was to be known as Beauty.

As a yearling, Dark Invader was seen and bought by the rich and spoiled young owner, Captain the Honourable Peter Hay, on the advice of his trainer Michael Traherne. It was a hefty price, but it was a well-bred colt and, "Having come to Dublin, Peter was going to buy something anyhow," Michael told his wife, Annette, "and this seemed a likely one."

The big youngster was shipped to the Traherne stables at Dilbury on the Berkshire downs where, lucky horse, he came under the care of that gnome of a stable lad, Ted Mullins. At the end of their career it was difficult to think of one without the other.

I

Every early morning of each racing season Mother
Morag, Reverend Mother of the Sisters of Poverty,
saw the string go by, a long line of horses, brown, dark
bay, bay: chestnuts – worst of all colours in the heat:
now and again a roan, or a blue roan: a grey, dappled
or flea-bitten. Mother Morag not only saw them, she
deliberately came up to her cell to watch them – her
window overlooked the road – but this was not Dilbury or England, not the mists and freshness of the
Downs where, in the wooded valley down below, the
village stood among trees, an uneven tumble of roofs
and chimneys round the grey church tower; there, the
first sound was the bird chorus, especially larks; here,
the first sound was the cawing of crows. In the cold
weather there was mist, but it swirled above arid dust,
because this was Calcutta in India and the 'string' was
not Michael Traherne's – Michael, friend of royalty
and other famous owners – it was John Quillan's, he
who had defiantly chosen to drop out. When Mother
Morag had first seen them in 1923 there were just
seven horses; now, ten years later, there were nearer
forty. Yes, John Quillan has made his way, thought
Mother Morag, simply because he's so good.

Racing news was relayed to her by the Convent's Gurkha gatekeeper, Dil Bahadur – Valiant Heart. "He has earned that name," Mother Morag often said. "Dil Bahadur has been through the War, fought in France and on the Frontier. Have you seen his scars and medals?" and she may have added, "Have you seen his kukri?", the wicked, curved, flat-bladed cutlass of the Gurkhas. Dil Bahadur shared Mother Morag's passion for horses. It was he who told her John Quillan's name. "John Quillan Sahib – was Captain Sahib, but not now," said Dil Bahadur.

Mother Morag had picked John Quillan out long before that. He always led his cavalcade down to the racecourse riding the stable 'steady', a bay mare that she guessed was his own. Mother Morag had noticed the grace with which his long leanness sat in the saddle, the quietness of his hands and voice – she never heard him shout at horse or groom or riding boy. She knew the old felt hat he wore where everyone else had topees; the, she discovered afterwards, deliberate shabbiness of his clothes; she even noted the signet ring on his little finger. A splendid pair of Great Danes, amber-coloured, loped each side of him. They struck terror into people but looked neither to right nor left and always sat by the side of the road until he gave the whistle to cross. "I wish I had your authority," Mother Morag was eventually to tell him.

"I wish I had yours." That had been open, friendly, and she told him how she watched his string and repeated, "You're so good."

"Good? Perhaps a little less disastrous than the other shockers." Then the 'shutter', as she was to call it, came down over his face. "Most of them though are ex-jockeys. I'm not and in this town that counts against me."

"Why?" Mother Morag's 'Why?'s were always direct.

"People know where they are with them; with me they don't, which is awkward for them."

"And for you?"

"For me?" He shrugged. "I'm as thick-skinned as a rhinoceros and I have ceased to care."

"I don't believe you. In fact, I think you care about your work as much as we care about ours."

"Touché," and, for a moment, he smiled. Then, with sudden seriousness, he had said, "We can't compare. I just play with rich men's toys unfortunately – or fortunately" – the mocking tone had come back – "Nabobs don't mind what they spend on their toys. The only rub is they want a sure return – of course. They're box-wallahs." A box-wallah is a businessman and Mother Morag felt sure that if she had not been there he would have said, "Bloody box-wallahs." "Horses can't be made to fit a ledger," said John Quillan.

Mother Morag had first met John when he, like others, had come to see her about the Convent's site.

Not all John's owners were box-wallahs; he had the Nawab of Barasol's horses and three of Lady Mehta's, that capricious owner and wife of the Parsi millionaire from Bombay who was always called Sir Readymoney Mehta because he let his exquisite Meena buy where and what she liked, "Unhappily," said John. She had given him many a headache. He also had two Aus-

5

tralians who, like many Australians, shipped horses every autumn to Calcutta's Remount Depot from their own stations in New South Wales; they also shipped their polo ponies and stayed for the polo season, selling the best afterwards, and John's two friends brought in four or five racehorses as well – or potential racehorses – which they left at the Quillan stables, but it was true that most of John's owners were businessmen of whom the British were the élite, "Or think they are," said John.

Calcutta has been a city of traders since the first small trading posts were set up on the swampy banks of the Hooghly, that great river up which, from the Bay of Bengal, first sailing clippers, then liners, paddle-steamers from inland tributaries, barges, and the age-old native country boats, unwieldy, wooden, with their tattered and patched sail or sails, and huge steering paddle would come, day in, day out, night in, night out – Calcutta never went to sleep – to deliver and load the cargoes that made those merchants so fabulously rich.

It was for those 'nabobs' – the men who so astutely dealt in jute – or tea – once upon a time in opium, or in hides, shellac, coal, jewels – that Indian landlords built mansions in ornate Palladian styles with porticos, vast rooms, deep verandahs, floors and stairways of imported marble. Each had lines of stables, coach houses, servants' quarters and courts, gardens like parks, and ignored the teeming slums which had grown up round them. A row of these great houses edged the L made by the Esplanade and Chowringhee, Calcutta's widest street; they fronted the

6

Maidan, the central space of open green, as the houses of London's Park Lane – once, too, belonging to magnates – front Hyde Park. Some spread into the streets that ran back from Chowringhee; others were built along the shaded roads that led to the rich suburbs of Alipore and Ballygunj and it was in one of these roads that, left to them by a long-ago plutocratic patron, the Sisters of Our Lady of Poverty had their convent and old people's home.

"What a waste," most people said. "What a waste!" "Which is why they so often came to see me," said Mother Morag.

It was certainly a favoured site, among the most pleasant of that unpleasant city. The Maidan was wide; it held the old British Fort, built isolated so that, if attacked, its cannon balls could rake the enemy on every side. Now, more peaceably, the Maidan held, not enemies, but the Football Club, hockey fields, two polo grounds and, divided from them by a road, the Victoria Memorial with its white marble domes and marble paved gardens where Calcutta's more prosperous citizens liked to walk in the cool of the evening. The Maidan had great tanks or pools, refreshing to sit by; several roads, yet there was still room to hold enormous political or religious meetings, and room for goats and the lean sinewy cattle to graze, for children to play, for beggars or pilgrims to camp; at night their insignificant twinkling fires shone far across its darkness. It had room still for riders and, most importantly, there was the racecourse with its stands, two courses and an inner circuit for work. Most important of all in that arid crowded city, there were trees, grass, above all space. On its far side the Maidan was bounded by the river, so that if there were any breeze, it was fresh.

"Such an expensive site," said the lawyers who were continually sent by their clients, most of them race-horse trainers, to see Reverend Mother Morag. "You're not four hundred yards up Lower Circular Road." Lower Circular Road, which led up to Ballygunj, abutted on Circular Road proper which ran past the racecourse. "The horses would only have to cross the road!" and it was not only the position; the Convent had many outbuildings which could be converted to stables. "Surely you don't need all those," and, too, there was the garden. "You can't need so much ground," and, "Think what you could sell it for!" they told her. "Think what you could do with the money!" Mother Morag was unmoved but they persisted in "pestering", she said.

John Quillan had only asked her once, though for him it would have been even more ideal than for the others; his own stables were just up the road and he badly needed to expand. The plan seemed sensible on both sides. "You could move further out," he told her – John had come himself and not sent a lawyer. "Move where land is cheaper so you could build just what you want," and he had asked, "Does it really matter where your Sisters live?"

"Of course it matters. Think." That took him back. "You'll have to mind your ps and qs," Bhijai, the young Maharajah of Malwa had told John – oddly enough that unreliable but charming playboy was a friend of Mother Morag's, as he was of John's, one of his few friends. "My father, the late Maharajah, knew her father," Bunny told him – Bhijai, like other young Indian fashionables, had adopted an English nickname. "When she came out here, her father asked my father to look after her. He died and so it fell to me, but as a matter of fact, Mother Morag looks after me. I often ask her advice," said Bunny. "I love her but she awes me."

"Which takes a bit of doing," John had teased him but, face to face with her, he understood the awe. He found that Mother Morag, though she seemed young to be a Reverend Mother, had surprising dignity. She was tall, almost as tall as he, though far too thin. He liked her poise, the clear bones of her face and the hazel eyes set off by the close white coif she wore. Her habit was white too and immaculately clean, though it was patched. There was another surprise; her eyes had lit almost with mischief when he mentioned Bunny and John saw why the two of them were cronies, but now she looked directly, almost sternly, at him and, "Not matter where we live? Think," said Mother Morag.

John knew, in part, what she meant. For most foreigners, whether they came from the West or Japan, Calcutta was a city of sojourn, where they made their pile, or did their service, government or military, then went 'Home'. "But not for us," Mother Morag said. "We are usually here for life." She could have added, "And I can guess, not for you." "Of course, it's by our own choice," she said aloud, "but remember nuns have no holidays, no 'leaves' and so, to keep ourselves healthy – and sane," she gave him a quick smile, "we need our haven." She did not tell him that they shared the haven with some two hundred others; it was reward enough to know that these old men and women, after their hard-working or starved neglected lives, could end their days in what seemed to them incomparable comfort and beauty, and Mother Morag smiled again as her eyes rested on the sight of the convent trees, gol-mohrs – peacock trees – and acacias, mangoes, jacarandas, that in spring and summer brought a wealth of flowers and fruit and where bright green red-beaked parakeets flew and played. "Also, has it occurred to you," she asked John, "that here we are near our work?"

That was true. The Sisters did not stay in their haven – they were to be found in the narrow lanes, alleys and gullies of the slums that made an intricate congested and evil web, inconveniently close behind Calcutta's elegant façade. If any flowering or fruit trees had been planted in those gutter streets, goats and bulls would immediately have eaten them; the bulls wilfully – plump, with hides like velvet, their humps capped with beaded coverings, lovingly embroidered, they ate what they chose, because to the Hindus they were sacred and must not be forbidden, "One of the endless taboos which make our work so difficult," said the Sisters. The goats ate because they were hungry, but not as hungry as the swarm of men, women and children.

In an Indian village, though people go hungry, they seldom starve; it is a virtue to feed the poor but in a city that virtue is quickly lost. "There are just too many of them," said Mother Morag. "We feed perhaps a thousand a day but it's a drop in the ocean. Still, it's a drop."

"I don't know how you manage it," said John.

"Nor do we, but we have our life-lines," said Mother Morag.

A necessary life-line of the Sisters of Poverty was Solomon, their horse. "If you can call him a horse," said Mother Morag. Sister Mary Fanny, the pretty little Eurasian, did not understand. "Is Reverend Mother trying to provoke us? I thought we all loved Solomon." Mother Morag relented. "Of course we do. I was only joking. He's so sturdy and reliable and more than that," she added.

Everyone knew Solomon; he was a cob – bright bay with white points, solid as if he were stuffed, "which he is," said Mother Morag. "All those tidbits."

Gulab, his old Hindu syce, groomed him until the coarse coat almost shone and polished the brass and leather of his harness so that no-one could have guessed how old it was; but it was not only his looks or that Solomon worked so hard in the cause of charity which made everyone love him; it was his expression, gentle and benign; the way he would let even the dirtiest gutter child pat him, the manners with which he accepted any kind of offering and, though he was slow, his dignified gait; he still moved with the arched neck and high-flung fore feet that showed he had been well trained to a carriage, "though I could never have believed a pair of hooves could have stayed in the air

11

so long without being brought down by the law of gravity," said Mother Morag.

The convent had two conveyances – they could not be called carriages; one was a high shuttered box on four wheels, the same as the tikka gharries – carriages for hire – of every Indian city but, being under Gulab's charge, better kept than they. It went out every afternoon, sometimes taking the Sisters in pairs to the business houses to gather in subscriptions and donations. For this Mother Morag sent younger nuns, Sister Bridget, plump and jolly, who could always make a joke, or Sister Joanna, the young English nun of strength and distinction but whose brown eyes, even when she did not say anything, could glow with indignation or be tender or laughing. The Sisters usually caught the men at their desks and, "It's hardly fair," said Sister Joanna. "Particularly the young ones, poor lambs. They don't know how to say 'no' to a nun."

"They know how to say 'no' to their tailor's and bootmaker's bills." Old Sister Ignatius, the sub-prioress and Mother Morag's right hand, was as tart as she was faithful.

On other afternoons Solomon would drive to the Newmarket, Calcutta's great covered bazaar, where the Sisters would pick up sacks of unsold vegetables from particular stalls; sometimes a few flowers for the chapel would be given them too, and while Solomon stood waiting in the forecourt, boys and girls would come to pet him and he would be given what Sister Bridget called 'goodies'.

"Yes. He too feeds from alms," said Gulab with

pride – to Indian thinking it is the receiver who has the merit, not the giver. At the side of the cart was a brass-bound collecting box with a cross carved on it and a slit through which brown hands – and sometimes white ones – put annas, the smallest silver coin, and copper pice – a pice was worth a quarter of an anna. There were even smaller coins: pies – like old time farthings – four to a pice, and even below these were cowries which still were currency, "But from that box you would be amazed how much we get," said Sister Emmanuel, the cellarer. "I think we often live on poor people's pennies." Solomon's real work though was the night round and for this he drew a cart not far removed from a bullock cart, heavy, with wooden wheels not properly tyred so that it shook and rattled. Its canvas hood made it seem like a covered wagon and its wooden seats were hard. It was the night round that took the heaviest toll of Solomon, Gulab and the Sisters.

In most Orders, the Rule is that its sisters must be in the convent by sunset but there have to be exceptions and for the Sisters of Poverty, in Calcutta's climate, to collect food during the heat of the day would have been a waste of time; kept standing in their canisters in hot kitchens it would have gone bad. "No-one else would have taken time to sort and cool it," said Mother Morag and so when, almost at first light, she looked down from her cell window to see the horses go by, she was already up and dressed and had been up since one o'clock because, as Superior, she made it her task to meet Solomon and his cart and the two Sisters who went with it on its nightly tour of the city's restaurants just as they were closing, to collect in the Convent's big battered containers the left-overs from dishes served to customers. "Some hardly touched," the Sisters marvelled. "To order such expensive food and then not eat it!" To them it seemed the height of riches.

"The height of gluttony!" Sister Ignatius was more than usually sharp-tongued. "It should be brought home to them."

"Then we shouldn't have the food." That was Sister Joanna with the remorseless logic of the young.

"Yes, see how out of sin comes good." Sister Mary Fanny was given to what Mother Morag called 'cuckoo-words' or platitudes. But in this case they were true. "How else would we feed our old people?" asked Sister Joanna.

"We, the Sisters of Poverty have always had a curious form of book keeping," Mother Morag was to tell John Quillan. "First we find the needy, the helpless ones, and take them in, then we find the means to keep them."

"Sounds crack-pot to me," said John. "How can you help people when you haven't the means?"

"Because the need is there and so, to fill it, the means come. They always have. Always," Mother Morag insisted, "if you trust. Almost a hundred years ago our foundress, Thérèse Hubert, who had no idea she was a foundress, used to take her basket and go round the houses of Bruges collecting scraps for the two old people she had taken into her tiny home. She got not only food but clothes, furniture, fuel."

"There were just two!' John objected. "Now?"

"At the last count, our Order of the Sisters of Poverty cares for more than fifty thousand old people. We have houses all over the world but, of course, in poor countries – or countries overburdened with poor, like India – it is more difficult. They don't want more beggars," Mother Morag smiled, "and we are, of course, beggars."

"Then what happens?"

"It still works. We believe we bring Providence by our very 'collecting', as we call it. It wakes people up, but don't think it's easy to beg. I remember Sister Joanna when she started: 'What would my father say if he could see me now?'" and Mother Morag spoke seriously. "You need to be very humble and disciplined, Mr. Quillan, to hold out your hand, to smile and say, 'God bless you', when doors are slammed in your face, when you are patronised or derided as nuisances – which, of course, we are." The smile had come back. "I sympathise because we're a continual reminder of what people don't want to know. I often wish we had orphans – so much more attractive than the old, but it's wonderful the way things do come. In her later years Thérèse Hubert told how, in one of the houses, when the old men and women had been fed, there was nothing left for the Sisters, but they still gathered round the empty table as is the Rule, and said Grace. There was a knock at the door; someone unknown had sent round an entire dinner."

"Just then?" John's face was half amused, half full of pity, but, "Just then," Mother Morag said firmly. "It's usually very prompt. It wouldn't be much use if it wasn't, would it?"

15

The night round was hard, not only on the Sisters but on Solomon and Gulab. Solomon often had to stand for half an hour – some of the restaurants seemed to take pleasure in keeping the Sisters waiting – and in the cold weather months, Solomon and Gulab shivered. Then it was on to the next place, often retracing the route because the kitchens were not ready.

The Sisters, too, often met with the contempt Mother Morag had spoken of; they had to wait in the outer kitchens, amongst squalid washing up, shoutings, horseplay. Sometimes waiters or cooks were drunk – the cooks more often. Mother Morag could never send young nuns on the night round. She sent Sister Timothea of the sharp elbows, Eurasian and, from a child, used to fending for herself, or Sister Jane, a truly plain Jane, or the French Sister Ursule who was hideous with warts on her nose, hairs on her chin and who wore spectacles like goggles. "No one is going to pester me," she said. Some places, though, were kind; the Italian head waiter at Firpo's always had a cup of coffee for the Sisters and many of the Indians had an innate respect for the religious; some even gave flowers from the vases on the tables, but seldom was the food properly separated in the canisters the Sisters left carefully labelled 'meat' 'fish' 'vegetables' 'curry' 'rice'. "Sometimes the food is thrown in so mixed that even we can't eat it," said Mother Morag, "but Sister Claudine, who is our cook, can turn most of it into gourmet food and it's lovely to see how the old people put on flesh and vigour. The trouble is they get so well that . . ." She stopped. "Of course I don't mean that. It's just that we're so over-crowded and there are so many waiting." She sighed.

When at last the cart came in, no matter how late or tired they were, the Sisters always gave Solomon the saved slice of bread and salt Sister Barbara the caterer had left ready; often, too, he had pieces of sugar-cane Gulab bought out of his own money. Then Solomon was walked away to be rubbed down, rugged in his old blanket and fed; Mother Morag sent the Sisters to bed and the heaviest work of the night began as another two began to carry the canisters in and sort the, by now, greasy food. "You cannot imagine what the smell of curry is like at two in the morning," Mother Morag told John. It was all carefully stored, either on ice or in the cool larder, and when that was done the canisters had to be scrubbed with disinfectant and hot water, then scalded. Often, seeing the Sisters tottering – they had usually worked all day as well – Mother Morag sent them to bed and finished alone. "It's a good thing I'm strong," and when, at last, she took off her big blue apron and the 'sleeves' that protected her white habit, she went upstairs to wash her face, neck and hands. Though it was probably only an hour or an hour and a half before the caller came round to wake the Community for the thirty-five minutes' meditation they had before Mass, it would have been sensible to have at least taken off her shoes and coif and lain down to rest her aching back and legs. "I'm not getting any younger," she told herself, but it was strangely more refreshing to sit at her window waiting till the string came by.

*

She could hear them before she saw them – a light drumming on the track and an occasional clinking of bits, swishing of tails, muttered words. Then they came, each beautiful animal swathed in rugs or horse-coats in the maroon of the stable colours; each was led by its own two syces or grooms, the men's heads swathed too in their chuddars – small cotton shawls of which one end was usually wound over their mouths and noses. They wore long coats of good cloth, braided with maroon, good shoes in keeping with the high rank of their charges. "I wish we could give Gulab a coat like that," the nun in Mother Morag could not help wishing. "These men don't have to go out on the night round," and then she forgot the nun in the sheer joy of watching the horses. Some moved steadily; some, more finicking and fidgety, curvetting and pulling, trying to shy at bits of paper or at an old woman sweeping up twigs on the road, had a riding boy atop as well, but all were kept in perfection. Where their flanks, shoulders and necks showed, these were glossy; their muscles rippled as they moved on legs slender and strong but, as Mother Morag knew well, vulnerable. All were led by John Quillan on his mare, Matilda, and each side the Great Danes, Gog and Magog. Mother Morag had learnt their names.

Dark Invader was two years old; far removed from the long-legged foal and the clumsy promising yearling. His coat now was a dark brown with a dapple in it. The proud curve of his neck was not yet showing the crest of his sex but the majestic slope of his shoulder, the great breadth and leverage of his hocks and his feet so well-shaped and firmly placed made him a handsome individual.

The day was celebrated by some extra carrots and half a pound of lump sugar. Ted would allow no more. "Never met such a greedy-guts." No one could have guessed from Ted's brisk strictness that Dark Invader was the glory of his heart. "Never had one quite like this, sir," he told Michael and, "You always say that," teased Michael but, "I have a feeling Ted might be right this time," said Annette.

"Well, I must admit I have seldom had a youngster that looked better." Michael was cautious but Peter Hay was "like a peacock with two tails," Michael told Annette, "and vain as a peacock," he could have said.

"We'll run Darkie at Lingfield," said Peter, "and get Tom Bacon to ride him."

"If we can," said Michael.

"*I* can," which was true; Peter could buy almost anything and, on his next visit, "Bacon will do it," said Peter. "He'll probably come down here. Should be quite a formidable combination, Darkie and Streaky." He rubbed his hands. "What do you think, Ted?"

Peter always tried to get on with the lads; the young ones admired his clothes and cars, but when it came to horses, "Not up to much" was the verdict and he never got as much as a ghost of a smile from Ted.

Ted Mullins was truly a gnome of a man, dried, weather-beaten, with a tuft of hair part white, part childishly fair. He looked far older than his forty-nine years but his watery eyes, blue as larkspurs, were continually alert for an order or the well-being of his horse.

"What's that chap's history?" Peter had said. "I've always meant to ask."

"Ted? I've known him for years, my father had him as a fifteen year old, went on to be a jockey – pre-war. I gather he never quite had the devil to be top class; sort you use to bring a horse on and replace on the big day. Remounts in the war, demobbed to find his wife dead of the 'flu, his racing contacts lost and a lot of up-and-coming youngsters competing for the few available rides. Found a job with a small trainer in the North who got warned off and Ted lost his licence. Then he didn't seem to care any more, nobody left to fight for and he wasn't important enough even at his best for anyone to want to fight for him. Whisky didn't help either," said Michael. "In fact I think he was killing himself with drink, then he remembered my father and I remembered the old man had thought a lot of him and of his wife, Ella."

"And so do you," said Peter.

"Best stable lad I ever had," said Michael warmly, "and I think he shouldn't be doing that, but he's back where he began through sheer bad luck, yet never grumbles. Still has an occasional bout, but keeps it and himself to himself. Rides work beautifully and has uncommonly good hands. Look what he has done with Darkie."

"I grant you that," and Peter tried the little man again. "What d'you think about Lingfield, Ted?" hoping at least for recognition but, "It's not for me to say, sir." Ted's wizened face was like a mask.

A few minutes later Peter had gone with a roar and broop-broop of his bright red latest Bugatti, and, "What *do* you think, Ted?" asked Michael, "about Bacon and Darkie?"

"Well, I s'pose it's a compliment, sir." Ted would say no more but after the trial gallop with Bacon he took the uncommon liberty of following Michael into the office and, "No, sir. Never," said Ted.

"No? I thought it was a success."

"Have you looked at the hoss?"

"Yes. Seems all right."

"Wasn't. Should have seen him when he come in and this was only a gallop. It's going to be a *race*, sir." Ted usually had few words but now he burst out, "Some hosses come on normal like, some too fast for their own good, as you well know, sir, but some is slow. The Invader," Ted never called his charge Darkie, "the Invader's one of those; it's not that he's green ezackly, he's too intelligent for that. P'raps it's because he's so big, intelligent-like, and he wants time to look and think."

"Come off it, Ted. Horses don't think."

"Most hosses. If 'twas *my* choice . . ."

"Are you being a bit of an old hen, Ted? Bacon's report was good. Darkie's in first class condition. Right time. Right age."

"I said if it was my choice."

Michael hesitated. "Captain Hay is set on it."

"Him." Ted's croak, harsh from years of wind, rain and sun – and whisky – was scornful. "Hosses, cars, boats, all alike to him."

Michael had to agree and sighed but, "Ted, horses

have to have owners," he said, "or there wouldn't be any racing."

"Owners have to have hosses or there wouldn't be any racing," answered Ted.

John Quillan came to see Mother Morag again. He brought Gog and Magog but left them at the entrance to the courtyard where they sat each side of the gates like two mammoth ornaments, greatly reinforcing Dil Bahadur's prestige. John himself went round to the front door and the portress showed him up to Mother Morag's office on the first floor where she was working with Sister Ignatius.

"I haven't come to pester you," said John.

"For which we're thankful," Mother Morag laughed, but asked, "Then why?" and John came straight to his business.

"You have a horse."

"Yes. Solomon."

"Of course I know him, but only one horse so I thought you might have stabling to spare and I have a new client, a Mr. Leventine."

"Leventine!" Bunny had expostulated. "Why to heaven are you taking on an outsider like that?"

"His horses." John said simply.

No-one could deny that Mr. Leventine had an extraordinary flair for horses, but his ebullience, his plump glossiness, his scent and over-dressing, the perpetual pink rose in his buttonhole – "Pink is for happiness," he often said, beaming – his curly auburn hair that, with his slightly dusky skin, looked strange to Western eyes, and his over-emphatic sibilants, "are a bit off-putting," admitted John.

"Johnny, how do you keep so lean?" John had to grit his teeth when anyone called him Johnny. "So lean!" lamented Mr. Leventine.

"Sweat," said John, "and I don't eat lunch at the Bengal Club." The Bengal Club had the best food east of Suez, especially their spiced hump of beef and a certain Greek pudding made of sago, palm sugar and coconut. It was also renowned for its cellar and its custom of a glass of Madeira after luncheon. Mr. Leventine did not lunch there either – anyone thinking of inviting him would have been quietly persuaded not to by the secretary, "as they would with me," John could have said, "for a different reason I hope," but his voice betrayed no feeling as he said to Mother Morag, "A Mr. Leventine. He is importing horses from England and France. I am pressed for room and I wondered if you would rent us a few stalls."

There was an embarrassed silence. Then Mother Morag said, "We have to put people in ours."

"And they don't have electric fans nor are fed five times a day," Sister Ignatius could not restrain herself. "They are only people, not racehorses."

"Sister, *please*," but John said, "I see, and I beg your pardon." He had turned to go and was almost at the door when Mother Morag called him back. "Mr. Quillan."

"Yes?"

"I understand your wife is a Catholic."

"Yes." He was ready to be defensive but, "We were wondering," said Mother Morag, "as St. Thomas's is

23

quite far, wondering whether she would care to come here, to our chapel, for Mass. We are so close."

The silence was so long she thought she had offended him, then, "This is the first time in this city of upstarts that anyone has called Dahlia my wife, or asked her to come anywhere," and John said, "Thank you."

"The children too, of course."

The 'shutter' came down at once. "That wouldn't do." John had a tribe of children who were a by-word in Calcutta. Dahlia, sweet and warm, loved babies but had no control over children, "and babies grow into children, unfortunately," said John. His were as good looking as he, or as pretty and peach-skinned as their mother with her great dark eyes and silky lashes but they were untamed, went barefoot, wore what they liked, and did what they liked. They could talk good English when they wanted – oddly enough they followed John's unconscious perfection, not Dahlia's chi-chi – but preferred to chatter in Hindu or Bengali. They ran away from every school they were sent to, "Sensible children," was all John said – he seemed curiously helpless over them. "Well, remember they are tainted with the Eurasian," said Sister Ignatius – in the thirties that was a real taint – "Even here," she said – the Sisters of Poverty had Eurasian as well as Indian Sisters – "amongst ourselves of course it makes no difference, but among our old people!" The most indigent Indian, the poorest white, kept himself apart and Mother Morag thought that John's habitual bitterness, his mordant humour and defensiveness was not for himself, nor for Dahlia – he had too much tenderness for her – but for his children whom he called the 'bandar-log' – the monkey people.

"Why wouldn't it do?"

"Dahlia tried to take them to Mass but they wouldn't dress properly."

Mother Morag could guess how shamed Dahlia would have been – many of her own people went to St. Thomas's. It was a church parade but, "We don't mind how people are dressed," said Mother Morag, "as long as they come. Bring them."

He looked so startled – and was it softened? – that she wondered if what she had said had somehow offended him and then wondered again if, perhaps, this was the first time he had thought of his 'bandars' as people. She did not know but, after that conversation, every month, without a word or a note, John Quillan sent his own farrier to shoe Solomon – without charge.

"I really must go and thank Mr. Quillan," said Mother Morag. "These are the third set of shoes."

"Well, take the umbrella," said Sister Ignatius. "It's still hot in the sun." It was not a true umbrella, but a sun-umbrella, too big to be called a parasol, of holland, lined with green, that the Convent had once been given, and Mother Morag was grateful for its shade as she walked up the road.

John lived in what had once been the country home of some eighteenth-century nabob, a graciously built house, which had been named Scattergold Hall because seldom had so much money been spent on a house and so quickly wasted. The town had caught up with it and it was surrounded, as was the Convent, by slums. Most of its once vast garden was now taken up by the stables, but there was still a tumble of flowers and tangled creepers, bougainvillaeas, tacomas, roses, jasmine; still massed flowery shrubs, lofty trees; still fountains, though broken, and empty pools. The house was of stucco with shuttered windows, some of the shutters now hanging askew. Pillars adorned and supported its wide verandahs and the porch had the height and width to take an elephant and howdah; broken brick had replaced the smooth gravel on the paths and carriage sweep, and geese, muscovy ducks and disreputable cocks and hens scratched and dusted themselves in a sea of red powder. There were rabbit hutches, pens for bantams and for guinea-pigs. "Papa gave us five and we have forty-two now," one of the bandars told Mother Morag. "We pretend we are shepherds driving our flocks." They drove them on what had once been the lawn.

The house smelled of cooking, particularly curry, and of a strange mixture of horses and flowers. Dahlia was no housekeeper; toys, saucers of food for animals, bowls of sweets and nuts, fans, her favourite magazines, snaffle-bits – polished and silver, that John was trying out – long whips and short whips, children's kicked off shoes, discarded topees, littered the rooms which Dahlia had furnished with comfortable chairs and sofas covered in a medley of brilliant chintzes, brass-topped tables, dhurries or Indian cotton carpets, "that can come to no harm," she said which, at least, was sensible – babies and animals relieved themselves anywhere. There were lamps with shades, fringed and tasselled; vases of paper flowers which she obviously prized far more than the pots of violets, lilies, carnations or chrysanthemums the gardeners set along the verandah; but for all the chaos Scattergold Hall was a happy place and many more people would have been glad to come if John had let them.

Mother Morag found him on the drive; Gog and Magog had let her in without demur, the Sikh gateman saluted her, and she was able to thank John in the name of the Sisters and of Solomon for the shoeing.

"Oh, that!" said John.

"Yes, that. Not only generous but imaginative," and Mother Morag said, "As I am here, may I call on Mrs. Quillan?"

"Mrs. Quillan?" The name seemed to give him almost a shock. Then, "Of course," he had said. "Dahlia will be delighted," and took her into the house. "I don't suppose," Captain Mack, the veterinary surgeon, told Mother Morag afterwards, "that an English lady had ever been in that house before."

"I'm not exactly an English lady," said Mother Morag. "I'm a Sister," and that was how Dahlia, in her simplicity, welcomed her except, "If I had known you were coming I should have dressed, m'n?" but the 'm'n' was said laughingly.

"I'm glad you didn't. I feel more at home." Dahlia wore heel-less embroidered slippers and a loose wrapper that gave a plentiful view of her warm peach and brown skin; her hair was loose on her shoulders. Mother Morag guessed that Dahlia dressed for an occasion could be a disaster but fortunately Dahlia had no ambitions except to make every creature, two-legged or four-legged, who came into her orbit, happy and comfortable, from the John she adored, through babies, children, horses, pet lambs, cats, mynah birds, Gog and Magog of course but, just as much, the pariah bitch who at that moment was having puppies under the verandah table, and she said to Mother Morag, "This iss verree nice," – a chi-chi accent is usually shrill, Dahlia's was soft. "And here, too, just in time, is our good friend, dear Captain Mack."

The bitch under the verandah table was being helped, or hindered, by four of the bandar-log squatting down beside her. They were worried. "Mumma, it's hurting her. It's hurting her terribly."

"She'll soon be better. See, Sandy has come, m'n." Dahlia soothed them and, to Mother Morag, "Captain Mack is a verree good friend to us."

"And to us," said Mother Morag.

The big red-haired freckled Scotsman was the official veterinary surgeon to the Turf Club, but he would turn out for a suffering pariah bitch as he would have to one of the Quillan, or any owner's, valuable blood horses, "and as he does often for us," said Mother Morag. For the Sisters it was the heartbreaking problem of dogs and cats. Not many of the old men and women, Indian, Eurasian, European, who came to the Sisters had pets, the struggle for their own survival had been too hard to allow that, but there were a few and, "I'm sorry we can't have your Moti," – 'Moti' meant a pearl – "or Toby or Dinkie," Mother Morag had to tell them. "We once had a poor bedraggled peacock," she said. "Bunny took him, and we have mynah birds. Fortunately we can take birds."

"But we're not an animal shelter." Sister Ignatius believed that if there had to be something painful, it was better if it were dealt with quickly, which often meant brusquely.

"But, Sister, I have had him for ten years. Couldn't you? For me? Mother, Sister, please. He would be just one."

"He wouldn't. He would soon be one of twenty."

Mother Morag would try and explain. "You see, if we have one, we have to have all. I'm sorry," – but it was Captain Mack who tactfully took Moti or Toby or Dinkie away and usually did not send in a bill. Now he hid his surprise at seeing Mother Morag and only said, "Out of the way, scamps, and let me have a look," as he knelt down beside the table.

John showed Mother Morag round the stables, "which is a real treat," and her face glowed. Gog and Magog dutifully rose to attend them, but first the children tugged at her habit, caught her hand, propelled her by the elbows to come and see their ponies, their own and others. The bandar-log were useful in schooling ponies, "belonging to other and better children," John said severely.

"Who can't ride and ruin their lovely little animals." The eldest bandar boy spoke so exactly like his father that Mother Morag could not help laughing, but she could see that this was serious; Quillans were always serious about horses and the children all rode, "like angels – or devils," said John.

It was the first time she had heard pride in his voice.

In contrast with the untidy ill-kempt house the stables were impeccable; the stalls, shaded by a verandah, ran round three sides of a square. Mr. Leventine had lent John the money to build the concrete block that filled the fourth side, a range of twenty up-to-date loose boxes, with water laid on, fans and ventilators, but still with verandahs and, John had insisted, roofed with old tiles – there were plenty from old outbuildings that had fallen down. "Must have cost near half a lakh of rupees," said Bunny.

"At six per cent." The bank rate was three or four. "But they wouldn't have given it to me without collateral, so six."

"*Six!* Leventine charged you six per cent! I told you he was a bounder."

"Not at all," said John. "He knew I had to have the money and he's nobody's fool. That, if you want to know, is me, but at least there's no hurry about paying it back."

The old stalls and verandahs were floored with brick; each, too, had an electric fan and, over the open fronts, guarded by wooden rails, hung rolled up khus-khus, thick grass matting blinds which were let down in hot weather and sprayed with water for added coolness. Each horse had its head collar hung beside the stall, its name above it. Mother Morag read them as she walked along: Ace of Spades: Rigoletto: Flaming Star: Flashlight – "Those two are Lady Mehta's," said John – Ontario Queen: Belisarius: The Gangster – "He's the Nawab's newest buy." The bedding had been put down for the night and across the front of each stall the grooms had made a thick plait of straw to prevent wisps coming out. The horses were tied outside ready for the evening grooming.

A track of tan ran round the square's central lawn which was green and smooth; Mother Morag could guess it was watered every day. There were white painted benches and chairs under its trees because it was here the owners gathered to watch the evening parade when the horses, groomed to perfection, were exercised round and round. "Exercised and scrutinised," said John. Now his foreman, the Jemadar, attended him and Mother Morag as they went from horse to horse and handed her, as the guest, appropriate tidbits for each, and heads came round and necks strained to catch them. One or two horses laid back their ears, showing the whites of their eyes, but John saw Mother Morag was not afraid. "There are always one or two bad seeds," she said; besides, the groom was always standing by to give a sharp slap of reproof. "Ari bap! Shaitan!" John's Matilda did not wait for them to come close, but started whickering at the sound of his footsteps. "Give her a banana," said John. "She'll peel it herself."

"What a beauty!" Mother Morag patted the satin neck. "Mr. Quillan, she's outstanding."

"Was. I had her in the regiment." Warmed by her delight, he unguardedly gave that fact away. "Not for racing, of course, for polo, but she's fourteen now." He ran his hand across her neck in a caress and again she saw the signet ring on his little finger, its worn crest. "Yes, we could do with some of your quality, couldn't we, old girl?" John said to Matilda. "Makes the rest look work-a-day squibs."

"Squibs! You have some splendid horses here, but
I'm intrigued," said Mother Morag. "Polo, then training racehorses. There's such a difference. How did
you come to know. . . ?" She stopped. "I'm sorry.
One shouldn't be curious, but horses run away with
you in more senses than one."

John Quillan was one of the few men she had met
who could look down on her and now he looked
almost with fellowship and, "How did I come to
know?" he said. "I can't remember a time when I
didn't. My grandfather, when he retired from the
Army, did a little breeding and training at Mulcahy,
our home in Ireland."

Mulcahy! He is one of those Quillans. Of course! I
ought to have guessed, thought Mother Morag, and
wondered if John had meant to tell her that. "My
father did the same, only more so, and my brother
decided to do it in a big way. Then . . ." The easiness
went and he said abruptly, "Came a time when I had
to do something – rather quickly; couldn't – didn't,"
he corrected himself, "go home. There was a trainer
here, an old Englishman called Findlay with a small
stable. He was good. As a matter of fact I had a horse
with him, just for fun. When it wasn't fun – the old
man was past it and needed a manager. He took me
on, for a pittance, but I was fond of him. He died the
following year and, well, I inherited and built it up
more or less."

"More or less! Bunny says you have win after win."

"Not the big ones."

"Why not?"

"They still won't give me the cream."

"Why?" The hazel eyes were so direct that he had to answer.

"Me, I suppose. So – no golden pots." He shrugged, but Mother Morag knew how much they meant: the Wellesley Plate: King Emperor's Cup: the Cooch Behar Cup and, crown of the season, the Viceroy's Cup, run on Boxing Day, and she laid her hand on John Quillan's sleeve; it was her left hand and, on its third finger, was her own ring, the plain golden band without crest or insignia, the sign of her wedding to Christ and the Church. "No golden pots."

"There will be, one day," said Mother Morag.

That evening Mother Morag had seldom felt as tired, perhaps because the visit to the Quillan stables had stirred up old memories, but the containers that night had seemed unusually heavy, greasier than ever, more smelly; also she could not get John Quillan out of her mind. "There will be, one day," she had prophesied.

"Dear Mother," he had smiled at her – for a hard sardonic man, John Quillan's smile was extraordinarily sweet. "Dear Mother. Always hopeful."

"Isn't that the purpose of my calling?" she had asked, and now, at her window, resting her tired arms on the sill, she wondered what was the quality that made someone, human or animal, one in ten thousand, or in a hundred thousand, stand out, not only because they were extraordinarily gifted, others are that, but because they seemed born with something extra, a magnetism that holds the public eye –

and the public love. Suddenly she seemed to smell broom in flower, golden broom, wet grass and horses sweating, to hear larks shrilling. Mother Morag was far from Calcutta; she had fallen asleep and what she had said was not, "There will be, one day," but, "One day there will be One."

II

That smell of broom in flower and wet grass filled the air as Michael Traherne rode with Peter Hay on the Dilbury Downs, and they heard the larks. Peter had spent the night with Michael and Annette and now the two men rode up over the tussocky grass, sparkling where it was brushed with dew in the sunlight.

Work was finished for the morning and, as they came up on to the high rolling uplands, far down the rough track they could see the lads putting the sheets back on the horses ready for the two-mile walk back to the stables in the village down below, whose roofs and church tower could be seen through the trees.

Michael was on his new young mare, a brilliant chestnut and still, each time she went out, as nervous as a dancer on her first night. Peter had settled for the stable cob. "I like them better when I'm off than on them," he had confessed.

They had come by a short cut, over the shoulder of the hill, the cob thumping along at a slow canter, the mare collected to match him until she shied at a rabbit, slewed round until Michael brought her back, held in perfect balance and flexing to the plain snaffle in tribute to his expert hand.

"Nearly had me off," Peter complained.

"You! Off our old dobbin? You couldn't be. Annette says he's a patent safety."

On the crest of the hill they halted, without speaking; then Michael broke the silence. "I think I have an offer for Dark Invader," he said.

"Have you so? Who, and how much?"

"Two thousand. A man called Leventine from Calcutta."

"Calcutta! Poor old Darkie."

"Not necessarily. Racehorses out there are treated like princes," but Peter was not listening.

"Leventine. Middle East, Jewish do you think?"

"I don't think so, could be anything. His full name is Casimir Alaric Bruce."

"Good God! That's not Jewish. What can he be?"

"Some sort of mixture. Immensely rich."

"Certainly seems to have more money than sense," said Peter. Michael let that pass. "What's his trade?"

"I don't know, but grandfather is said to have made a million."

"Jewels? Hides? Tea? I know," said Peter. "His grandfather was the man who first imported umbrellas into India."

"In that case Leventine would be a multimillionaire. May be for all I know. He doesn't give anything away. The 'Bruce' suggests some Scots in him which probably makes him cautious, yet he's a simple soul – somehow wistful."

"*Wistful!* My dear Mike!" but, "Yes," said Michael. "I think horses are his dream and he's coming up to be one of the most important owners in India, bar one or two Rajahs or Bombay magnates."

"But as a man?"

"Impossible, but I liked him. He first came over here two years ago, obviously a revelation, as was France."

"Can you see him at Longchamps?"

"I did and again this year. This time he was recognised by the Aga Khan – just."

"Strewth!" said Peter. "But in Calcutta?"

"Not even on the fringe of course, but he doesn't seem to mind. Why should he? He's a member of the Turf Club and on the way to becoming a racing personality; be a Steward before he's finished. Mr. Leventine knows exactly what he wants."

"And now he wants our horse. I wonder why."

"I imagine he's after what the people out there call the 'classics'," said Michael. "The Open Races of a mile and upwards; is ignoring Darkie's form and going by the way he's bred."

"And that, of course, puts him at the top of any class – but what has the brute done?" Peter's tone was suddenly wrathful. That young man's so spoiled he resents being let down by a horse, thought Michael, instead of taking it as the luck of the day. "What has he done?" asked Peter. "Nothing. Nothing since that win at Lingfield."

Lingfield. They were both quiet for a moment. Michael was thinking of the big dark two year old, left flat-footed at the start, then taken to the front by his long stride, collared just inside the distance by his better knit contemporaries, then coming again to win a fighting finish by a neck. "Superb riding by Bacon," said Peter.

"At least we thought it was superb," and Michael's puzzlement was shown as he said, "It's not as if Darkie had been cut to pieces."

"You said he hadn't a mark on him."

"Nor he had, but Bacon doesn't need to do that. Remember that second race at Doncaster?"

"I was away. Ascot."

"You would be." Michael did not say it but went on, "Darkie put Bacon over his head and bolted for the stables."

"Was Streaky hurt?"

"Not he. Indestructible, but he didn't like it. Of course, two year olds dump their jockeys on occasions, but this was different, as neat and determined a performance as I have ever seen. Same at Newbury only that time he wouldn't let Streaky even mount. In fact, I'm beginning to agree with Ted," and Ted's words echoed in Michael's mind. " 'Tisn't the Invader, sir. There's nothing wrong with the hoss. It's that Streaky. Streaky as they come," but, "Ted!" Peter was contemptuous. "That little runt! Still soaking it up?"

"Actually not," said Michael. "Ted hasn't had a breakout since you bought Dark Invader. When Ted has a purpose . . ."

"Some purpose! Mike, you know all Ted's geese are swans."

"Ted knows a swan when he sees it," Michael was steady, "and I believe he's right. Streaky can do something to a horse. Darkie wouldn't eat properly for a week after that first race and you know what a glutton he is."

"I think you believe," said Peter, "that Darkie has

it in for Bacon personally. It wasn't just racecourse nerves?"

"No doubt about it. It showed again here at home. Streaky came down to try a gallop, and Darkie was all over the place; wouldn't let him get near and we all had the hell of a time with him, sweated for hours afterwards. Ted nearly dropped walking him up and down."

"What did Streaky do?"

"Just laughed."

"He would. He doesn't have to worry about a recalcitrant youngster. Just has to 'say so' and any ride is his."

"All the same, he didn't like it. That laugh wasn't pleasant," said Michael. "I have never had any time for the man since, but what it adds up to is that Darkie reckons if he goes to the front he gets some almighty sort of punishment, physical or mental, so he wisely stays behind."

"Which is no good to me," said Peter. "Two thousand is a damned good price for a dog of a horse and that is what I am afraid he is."

"We could run him over hurdles," Michael suggested. "That sometimes does the trick. If he responded he might go back to the flat in handicaps or you could have him cut and send him over fences. He's big enough."

Peter was silent, then, "To be frank, Mike, I don't feel like spending any more on him. I was going to tell you that."

Michael did not answer; instead, "Look, here they come," he said, and he became suddenly silent, his

39

gaze concentrated on his charges. They were coming nearer, all walking well except the fillies Tarantella and Bagatelle, jiggling as usual. Now they were past and there was Dark Invader coming into sight.

Michael turned to Peter. "Here's our problem child. Frank says he walks so fast on the way home that he sets all the others jogging, so he has taken to sending him home separately. That only goes for the return journey. Going out you can hardly kick him along."

"Idle devil! But he certainly can walk when he wants to. Look at him now."

All horses can walk – some badly, some well, but to a few is given a gift of movement feline in its grace, a slouching flowing continuous motion that is a joy to watch. Dark Invader, blissfully ignorant that his fate was in the balance, strode in glorious rhythm, his great shoulders rolling, muscles rippling along his flanks under the satin skin, his simple mind concentrated on one single thought – breakfast.

"Here a minute, Ted." Ted swung the tall horse off the track and halted.

"Well, Ted, how's he going?" asked Peter.

"First class, sir," Ted said it stiffly.

"Keen?"

"Keen enough. Galloped a treat. And such a gentleman with it," and Ted said defiantly, "He's a bloody lovely hoss, sir."

"Ted's not far wrong at that, you know, Peter," said Michael. "Just look at him."

Resigned to the interruption of his journey, Dark Invader was standing quite still, interesting himself in the sights and sounds of the awakening countryside. His ears were a little long for a thoroughbred, and loosely set. They would lop sideways in moments of rest, contentment or embarrassment. Now they were pricked, eager and active, moving to catch the distant sounds and the voices around him and he seemed the portrait of a thoroughbred horse.

"He certainly fills the eye," said Peter and Ted burst out as he had once to Michael, "There's nothing wrong with the Invader, sir. It was that Streaky. Streaky as they come. He . . ."

"Happens to be one of Britain's top jockeys," Peter said icily. "If he can't manage Dark Invader no-one can."

Sitting on the big horse, Ted was able to look down on Peter, which he unmistakably did, and if Peter's tone was icy, so was the look on Ted's face, icy and disdainful. Then, "Will that be all, sir?" he asked Michael.

"Thank you, Ted," and Ted wheeled the Invader round and rode away.

Peter was slightly disconcerted, then quickly recovered himself. "The trouble is, Mike, a splendid conformation's no good without guts. We have to face it. Darkie is a great big beautiful washout."

Back in the yard they dismounted, and the horses were led away; all the lads' eyes were on Peter's car, a new black Sunbeam 3 litre, with the cycle-type front wings and slightly backswept radiator of the marque. Peter had already put his suitcase in the back.

"Well, what do you want me to do?" Michael asked abruptly. "I must give Leventine an answer."

"I don't think that 'chasing idea is any good," said Peter, "and, as I said, money's a bit tight. Besides I have decided to winter abroad, so . . ."

"So?"

"Sell him, Michael. No good getting married to the brutes."

"Very well, I'll do that. How d'you like your new toy?" Peter missed the sarcasm, answering seriously, "Goes well enough – but it hasn't the character the old 30/98 had." He swung his legs over the side of the low open body, ignoring the vestigial door. The car started with a roar then settled to the usual muted bass mutter of a wide exhaust.

"So long." Peter raised his hand in salute.

The lane resounded with the crescendo of his going. Michael listened for the last triumphant gear change at the turning into the main road. Then he walked heavily into his office.

The voice on the telephone was harsh and imperious, like the quacking of a vast and rather angry duck. Into the little cluttered room with its files of forage bills, tattered copies of the *Calendar* and *Ruffs Guide*, crumpled entry and declaration forms for race meetings long past, came a breath of world markets, of wide halls where tens of thousands could change hands at a shouted word or the mark of chalk on a blackboard. Yes, Mr. Leventine was still a buyer (quack), if the price wasn't right, Mr. Leventine would spring another five hundred, but that was his last word. (Quack?) It was a deal? (Quack?) Subject to vet's examination (quack). Some of his new horses were being shipped out soon and there was a box to spare. Michael could expect his veterinary surgeon next day. Mr. Leventine's cheque would follow as soon as the certificate was in his hands. Short credits long friendships – laugh – (quack, quack), silence.

"You'll have to tell Ted."

Breakfast with Annette in the house's warm dining-room was for Michael the best part of the day; cold and hungry after the dawn start and three strenuous hours' work, a plateful of porridge and cream, then bacon and eggs, hot toast and marmalade and his own outsize cup of coffee usually seemed like heaven, but this morning he had left the yard without a glance at the end stall where Dark Invader was craning his neck for attention and for an apple, or a few of the lumps of sugar Michael kept in his pockets. "A sale is a sale, all in the day's work," he told himself, but he seemed to see Darkie's future with a horrible certainty; the horse hated racing; he would be a total failure and would finish flogged to death in the shafts of some ramshackle carriage for hire or even a cart. Michael pushed his plate away.

"Have some more coffee," said wise Annette and, when he had the steaming cup, holding it in hands that still seemed to be cold, she said gently, "Tell Ted before he hears it from anyone else."

"As a matter of fact," said Michael, "Ted's part of the deal. He's to take Darkie out."

"Ted! To Calcutta!"

"If he will. It's one of Leventine's conditions. He seems to have been thorough in his enquiries," and Michael quoted: "'As the horse is temperamental, I should be glad if you would allow his own lad to make the voyage with him.'"

"What did Peter say to that?"

"What do you think? 'Who pays?'" Peter, who never had to worry; who always knew where the money to pay the stable bills would come from, yet could not spare the expense of keeping Dark Invader a little longer. "No, you're being too dramatic," Michael told himself but, wintering abroad, a new two thousand quid car – same price as for the horse – Peter, who had said before he had driven off, "Spending all that on Ted, Leventine might be good for another few hundred. See if you can sting him, Mike, but don't lose the deal," and, "*Owners!*" Michael was going to say it savagely, but Annette cut across. "This Mr. Leventine – he will do that for the sake of the horse. I think I like Mr. Leventine."

"But will Ted go?" asked Michael.

"In'ja," said Ted. "*In'ja!* You mean you're sending the Invader all that way? 'Mong all them heathens," said Ted in anguish.

"They're not heathen, Ted, but yes, India and not only him – you."

"Me!" For perhaps the first time in his life Ted's voice was shrill.

"Mr. Leventine," said Michael, "has asked that, to give Darkie the best possible chance, his own lad should take him out. His own – which means you."

"Strewth!" said Ted. The voice had become almost a whisper. "To Calcutta?" asked Ted.

"To Calcutta."

There was a silence. Then, "You mean this gentle-man," it was seldom Ted used that word, "this gentle-man will pay my ticket there and back?"

"There and back, and pay you."

"Just so as the Invader's not upset?"

"That's it."

"I'll go," said Ted.

III

Papers in hand, John Quillan waited on the quay of King George's Dock while cranes swung the horses ashore.

"There's one mitigating thing about Darkie," Michael had told Annette. "He'll be going to John Quillan."

"John Quillan?" Annette was startled.

"He's Leventine's trainer."

"*John?* A trainer in Calcutta! *John!* But isn't he in the Queen's Own?"

"Was. Should have had his majority by now."

"John has left the regiment?" Annette, herself a Colonel's daughter, could not believe it; not the John Quillan she had known in her twenties, danced with, ridden with, watched play polo. And, "Why?" demanded Annette. "Why?"

"There was some blow up. Pity. John was the younger son, but he was sitting pretty. Some exalted uncle or godfather must have been watching over him – expect gave him an allowance. I believe that when it happened John was A.D.C. to the Governor of Bengal."

"Calcutta in the winter. Darjeeling in the hot months." Annette knew the ritual.

"Yes. Could have been one of the chosen ones, silly idiot, until . . ."

John Quillan could remember that day. The Governor's Military Secretary, Colonel Maxwell, had sent for him.

"Sit down, John."

"Thank you, Max."

"His Excellency," – the Colonel did not say H.E., which showed the formality of the occasion – "His Excellency has decided that you should go on immediate leave. *Home* leave," the Colonel emphasised that point, "and on your return you will rejoin your regiment."

Silence. Then, "I don't have to tell you why," said Colonel Maxwell.

John had met Dahlia at a party, a 'B' party. "In this salubrious city," Robert Kerr, a fellow A.D.C. had said to John, then a newcomer to Calcutta, "there are A and B girls, the latter for the hot weather only – naturally most of ours go Home then."

"I see," said John. "What happens at the party?"

"Usual thing. They behave very well and we behave very badly and then they behave worse."

Dahlia, then eighteen, had been brought by her cousin, cajoled into it – "They need more girls" – and had sat terrified in a corner in her overbright cheap net dress, a little fish out of water; indeed, every now and then she gave a little gasp and her eyes, not confident, nor even interested, were like a sea anemone's that drop their fringes against the next wave they see coming.

47

John had taken pity on her. "You're not enjoying this."

"Oh yess. Yess," but he knew she meant, "No, no."

"Let me take you home."

A sharper gasp. Dahlia had been warned about those five little words.

"You mean – my home?"

"I mean your home," and she had trusted him.

"At least," he told Mother Morag, "she has trusted me ever since."

Even then John had been disgustedly against "the hypocrisy and callousness of this hateful city," he told Mother Morag. "The endless protocol and snobbishness of Government House; come to think of it, of my own regiment," and he had defiantly made friends with Dahlia's father, an Irish Eurasian mechanic on the railway who had married an Indian woman. John had liked Patrick McGinty and his big calm wife and was soon openly calling for Dahlia and protecting her at the parties to which he still went – "from monsoon boredom, I suspect." Dahlia had also been wonderfully pretty, with a dew of innocence that touched John's heart and often, in his car, they escaped into the night where, between deluges of rain, the drenched spaces of the Maidan were dense and dark as velvet and there was no one to see them except, when the clouds parted, stars big as sequins of Indian gold, and, nestling in his arms, Dahlia was sweet and, unlike other Calcutta women, absolutely without guile. "How many people are that?" John asked Mother Morag and, "She wanted me so badly," but he could not say that to a nun.

He had been warned by the young but more experienced Robert, "Don't get too enchanted, John. It can be expensive, you know."

"Expensive?"

"If you have to buy them off – for a reason," said Robert.

John had been warned off too, surprisingly, by Dahlia's father. "We would please ask you, Captain Quillan, not to take our daughter Dahlia out any more.'

"Why not?" John had been furious but Mr. McGinty was not intimidated.

"Dahlia is our only child. We think she is beginning to love you very much and we know, and you know, what happens to girls like Dahlia."

"You don't know anything," John had said, "about this."

"Don't we? You are Captain Quillan of a famous regiment. Also you are A.D.C. at Government House. As soon as your superiors hear, conveniently you will be sent back to England. In our world we are used to broken promises and broken hearts, but please not for Dahlia." Mr. McGinty was not angry, only sad.

John was silent, then he asked, "Do you play chess, Mr. McGinty?"

"Chess?"

"Yes. In chess there are Kings and Queens, Bishops, Knights – I'm not any of those – and pawns that can be moved any way the player likes. I am not a pawn, Mr. McGinty."

"We have booked you a sleeper on the Blue Train tonight," said Colonel Maxwell. "*Tonight*, John. You sail on the *Orion* next Tuesday. His Excellency has written to your Colonel."

"He could have saved himself the trouble," said John. "I have written to him myself. Sent in my papers."

"John!"

"You see, I married Miss McGinty this morning."

"You *what*?" and then, as Max took it in, "You young fool!"

"Exactly the congratulation I thought I should get," said John.

"He *was* a bloody fool," Michael told Annette. "No doubt about it; he could have paid the girl compensation, if he felt he had to do, as dozens of others have done. Maybe she had started a child, but he was let out of it already. Think, Annette, his father, grandfather, great-grandfather were all in the regiment, but John was always uncommonly quixotic."

"Or uncommonly honourable. Odd," said Annette. "He always seemed so cynical and yet I remember him getting angry about things the rest of us just accepted, and I think," said Annette, "though he kept it hidden, he was the kindest young man I knew."

On the quay this morning of October the sun was already hot. John's bush shirt was sticking to his back, he could feel the sweat on his neck running down from the band of his felt hat. Dahlia would have liked him to wear a topee – to her the mark of the true English – she was always running after the bandar-log with the topees they too refused to wear, "and come to no harm," said John.

Other trainers were waiting too but, after the first greeting, they kept apart. His, and their, Indian grooms, waiting to meet their new charges, squatted, gossiping and smoking; a hookah was passed round or biris, the small strong-smelling Indian cigarettes, were offered; some of the men chewed betel. An owner came down, obviously on his way to the office to speak to the popular Australian trainer, Dan Regan. He nodded to John then turned his back.

On the railway siding a gang of twenty brown-skinned crop-headed bare-footed men in dirty loin-cloths formed up behind a closed iron goods wagon. Another brown man wearing a coat shouted an order and the gang broke into a chant: "*Hull* a lai, *Hull* a lai." The wagon wavered, swayed and began to move.

Somewhere invisible a kite called kee-ee-ee, a sound seemingly unending, infinitely remote.

"God! What ages they take," thought John.

Dark Invader and Ted had been shipped with a dozen other racehorses by the *City of London* from Birken-head. It had been a cold, dark, drizzling day and now, a month later, the ship moored in warmth and sunlight to discharge passengers at a jetty in a broad river where kites swooped for floating offal and fought aerial battles with shrill mewing cries. Leaning over the rail with the other grooms, Ted saw the domes of a great building in dazzling white marble, brooding over a wide expanse of grass and trees.

"Thought it would be all dry and brown and dirty," said Ted. "Look, there's flowers," and there were white people, some of them riders among the flotsam of Indians; motor cars drove past and in the distance was an English-looking church with a spire, and Ted saw what made his eyes light up – the familiar white rails of a big racecourse. "Doesn't seem such an outlandish place as I thought," Ted had said.

The horses and grooms were not to get off here, and next day the ship dropped down the river to the docks and the cranes swung the horse-boxes ashore. "At long last," said John.

The horses walked out of their boxes, stepping gingerly on overgrown shoeless feet under the hot sun. The light was a bright glare and some of them held back, their lads holding them short on the leading rein, being jerked half off their feet. The Indian grooms ran to help them.

Seven of the newcomers were for John Quillan. Two were Lady Mehta's, five for Mr. Leventine. With Lady Mehta, John could not guess what he would get; spending every summer in France, she bought as she fancied. "It's no use advising Meena," Sir Prakash – Readymoney – Mehta said. "She was born wilful." Now John saw a mare – light bay, silky mane, lustrous eyes, a lovely appealing thing but, "Back at the knees," groaned John, "narrow-bodied as a board on edge." He flipped over the papers to find the vet's certificate. 'Sound', written aggressively in green ink. "You might have been then, you may be now, but you won't be in a year's time." John tried to keep the pity out of his voice as he patted the silken head. The next was better, a solid dark bay with the broad, well-muscled quarters of a sprinter. "Thank God we can do something with you," but John's real interest was in Mr. Leventine's five, his first experience of what that enigma would buy.

Two mares, a gelding and a young colt, sharp little horses good for races of six furlongs to a mile. Sound legs and good feet, bright-coloured coats, even after a long voyage and little or no grooming. The stuff to turn out week after week in the Winter handicaps, to stand the stifling heat and the bashing of the raised course in the Monsoon meetings. No-nonsense types, thought John. His respect for Mr. Leventine increased.

Last out of his box, overtopping the others by a hand, was Dark Invader. John looked at his papers. Leventine couldn't have bought this one, surely? But there it was: 'Brown colt, off hind fetlock partly white.' No mistake about that. Seventeen hands at least, thought John, too big for the Course. John looked at the paper again; unplaced since a win first time out eighteen months ago. John frowned. He wouldn't have thought Mr. Leventine would have thrown money away. Then, "Good morning, sir," said a hoarse croaking voice, and John found himself looking down at a little man whose blue eyes were appraising him – from head to toe, thought John. The polite 'Good morning, sir,' was quite unlike the 'Hy-ah', or 'Hullo there', of the other travelling grooms who relinquished their charges with a pat, sometimes even without a backward glance, as they went off with the trainers to collect their pay – and blow it during their few days in Calcutta, thought John. Why not? Their fares home were paid.

In contrast to their sloppiness, this little man was spruce in a clean shirt with a celluloid collar such as John had not seen for years, a waistcoat with a silk watch chain – probably made for him by his wife or admirer, thought John – cord breeches, box-cloth leggings and worn but brilliantly polished boots; those boots sent John back on a wave of almost unbearable nostalgia to his father's stable yard and the standards he knew now he had lost.

There was even the inevitable cloth cap, touched respectfully by the finger of one hand; the other hand held the big horse with an authority that kept the Indian grooms back.

"You must be from Mr. Traherne." Emotion always made John terse.

"Yes, sir. The name is Mullins. Ted Mullins."

"And I'm John Quillan. I train for Mr. Leventine."

"Yes, sir, and this is Dark Invader."

If Ted had expected eulogies he did not get them. John Quillan walked slowly round Dark Invader, appraising the horse as closely as Ted had appraised him. "Certainly fills the eye," was all he said, exactly as Peter Hay had done. That was too much for Ted and, in his turn, he said what he had told Peter. "He's a bloody lovely hoss, sir, and such a gentleman with it."

The horse was not the only gentleman. "Would it be in order with you, sir, if I walked the Invader home?"

John noted the use of the word 'home'; evidently Ted's appraisal had ended in approval, but John had to hesitate. "It's a longish walk, all of three miles."

"Good. After tramping round and round them decks the Invader'll feel a bit strange. He's used to me."

"Of course, but . . . would you just walk with him?"

Ted flushed. "You mean out here an Englishman shouldn't be seen leading a hoss?" He was nettled.

"It's a question of prestige, yes, but not yours," said John. "I'm thinking of Sadiq and Ali who will be Dark Invader's grooms – we call them 'syces' out here. Sadiq is waiting to take charge and if he doesn't . . . well, there would be a loss of face."

"I see, sir. Would he – Mr. – is it Saddick, sir? Would he mind if I walked along?" asked Ted.

Ted never forgot that first walk in Calcutta.

Sadiq was a head taller than Ted, the turban he wore making him seem even taller. He was burly – would have made two of Ted, dark with a fierce upturned moustache and prominent brown eyes with curiously yellowed whites, so that they reminded Ted of snail shells; already they were looking at Dark Invader with the pride of a mother in her first-born son and Ted had to swallow and turn his head away.

"You'll need a hat," John Quillan was saying. "That cap's no good. The sun is hot even though it's October. Perhaps you bought a topee at Port Said?"

"Didn't think it was worth it, sir, seeing as I'm going straight back." John noticed, too, that Ted's face was white.

"Sure you want to walk? All right, I expect I have a topee in the car – my wife puts one in."

A second groom had joined Sadiq on the off-side. Dark Invader led the way, the other Quillan horses coming behind but, even with the stiffness that came from the weeks of being boxed, his great stride soon outpaced them. "Him fast." Sadiq prided himself on his English.

"Ji-han!" the other groom panted as he tried to keep up. Ted was glad to see neither of them jerked on the reins. He put a restraining hand on Dark Invader's bridle. "Steady, boy, steady."

"S-steady. S-steady." The s's hissed through Sadiq's teeth.

Their way led, at first, through streets lined with one-, or two-, or three-storied houses, ramshackle, most of them hung with notices in Hindi and English, 'Malik Amrit Lal Patney, advocate' 'Goodwill Electric Company' 'Happiness Coffee and Tea House', alternating with shacks and open-fronted shops. Each street seethed with traffic – trams, buses, carts drawn by heavy white bullocks or even heavier massive wide-horned black water-buffaloes at whom their drivers shouted; Ted shuddered as he saw how the men cruelly twisted their tails and the sores, rubbed raw, on the bullocks' necks. Queer high box carriages passed, shuttered and closed, with a clatter of hooves and bumping wheels, and again he was sickened by the thinness, rubs and sores of the horses that drew them, some no more than ponies; though they wore strings of blue beads round their necks, and some had aigrettes of feathers in their browbands, their ribs and hip bones stood out, and some were lame but driven on with whips. The trucks had jewellery too, hung with tassels, as did some of the cars and taxis, with turbanned black-bearded drivers who seemed never to stop sounding their horns; now and again a shining well-kept car slid through, with perhaps one person in it and a smart, capped or turbanned chauffeur, but each taxi seemed to hold a dozen people and there were rickshaws, laden too, each with a skinny little man, glistening with sweat, running between the shafts and sounding the clank clank of its flat bell and, around and among them, on the pavements and in the gutters and in the road itself was a river of people.

Ted had never seen so many people, brown-skinned, some in only a loin-cloth, like those men on the dock, but here pushing loads on carts or with yokes balanced across their shoulders, or on their heads, women too, balancing a pitcher or a basket, or even a bucket, with a poise he could not help admiring. A few men were dressed in immaculate flowing white, a loose shirt, draped muslin instead of trousers, slipper shoes, and carried umbrellas and briefcases – Ted was to meet one of them, John Quillan's office clerk, or babu, Ram Sen – but babies were naked except for a charm string; they crawled on the pavements. Some of the boys were naked too, with swollen stomachs, and it seemed people lived in the streets; Ted saw women washing themselves under the street tap; true, they were wearing a sari, but the thin cotton, wet, showed every curve. A man, squatting on the pavement, was having his head shaved; another was dictating a letter; the letter writer had a desk, without legs, on the ground. Men turned their backs and relieved themselves in the gutter and Ted saw women slapping cakes of dung – yes, manure! thought Ted, astounded – to dry on walls; it was only afterwards he learned dung was used as fuel. Pigeons picked grain from the grain shops, pai dogs nosed rubbish and everywhere was a hubbub of voices, creaking wheels, motor horns, shouting, vendors' cries, mingling with a smell of sweat and urine, woodsmoke, acrid dung smoke and a pungent smell that later he was to learn came from cooking in hot mustard oil and, now and again, a waft of heavy sweetness as a flowerseller passed, or from a garland of flowers hung on a door, or from a woman in a clean, softly flowing sari, with flowers round the knot of her hair. Ted saw that between her short bodice and her waist, her midriff was bare and, What would Ella say? he thought; already his tuft of hair was standing on end and he was shocked to the depths of his clean Methodist soul – this is a dreadful place – yet, at the same time he was fascinated, so curiously drawn that he almost forgot Dark Invader.

Dark Invader though, with his customary calmness, passed unruffled; he did not know it, but this was his first encounter with his public.

*

Ted was more than glad when they left the streets and the hordes of people, to strike off across the green turf he had glimpsed from the ship. "Maidan," said Sadiq and here again were the white rails of a racecourse, well kept lawns and paddocks.

They passed mounted policemen, Englishmen in white uniforms and Indians in khaki. In the distance Ted saw mounted troops, the glitter of swords and the flutter of pennoned lances; a parade was going on but Sadiq turned away to the right, crossed a wide busy road and led the way up another, quieter, tree-shaded, with broad verges on which the horses' hooves made only a light sound. As they turned in through two huge open gates, once painted green, Dark Invader went still faster as if he knew he was coming to what Ted had called it – home.

"Good Lord," said Ted. "Good Lord!" It was the first time he had seen Indian syces grooming.

He had seen Dark Invader into a roomy stall, open-fronted, fenced in by two wooden rails, seen what a good feed was waiting, not in a manger as in England, but in a heavy galvanised tub, seen the crows, big black and grey birds with strong beaks and darting pirate eyes, fly down to perch on the rails, waiting for droppings of corn. They were, John Quillan told him, every horse's constant companions. Then Ted had gone with John. "I have booked you into the Eden boarding house. It's supposed to be good. I hope it is." After a lunch, when Ted was waited on by two table servants and, out of curiosity, tasted curry for the first time – he hastily ordered roast mutton instead – exhausted by the, to him, heat and strangeness as much as by the long walk, Ted had slept in his spacious room until John had come to fetch him. "Thought you might like to see my string."

Ted had blinked at Scattergold Hall, blinked more at the sight of the bandar-log; two were fighting over a large pet ram which, in its turn, was fighting them; one, a girl, was swinging like a monkey on a branch of a tree. An older boy was earnestly schooling a pony, while two, almost babies, were making mud pies on the edge of the drive, pouring red dust and water on each other's heads. Dahlia, in a rocking chair on the verandah and wearing her usual loose wrapper, sat peacefully rocking and fanning herself with a palm-leaf fan. She smiled over the fan at Ted with her dark fringed eyes and called "Hullo."

"My wife and children," John had said absently. Ted took off the topee John had lent him and bowed, but John did not introduce him; instead, "Come and see the horses and our evening grooming." He had led Ted to the stable square and Ted blinked again; more than blinked. He had never seen anything like it.

The horses were tethered outside their stalls to rings set in the wall, the syces, two to a horse, ranging themselves one each side. As Dark Invader was so big, Sadiq and the second groom, Ali, stood on upturned food boxes, set far back so that they could throw their weight on their hands, then laid into him with what John told Ted was the classic hand-rubbing – 'hart molesh' in Hindi – of Indian horse care. "You mean they groom with their *hands*?" asked Ted.

"Every part of their hands, fingers, thumb, the ball of the thumb, the heel of the hand and right up to the forearm. Watch."

Now and again Sadiq or Ali turned to rinse hands and forearms in a bucket of cold water to wash off the dead hair, then sweating and panting, back again, while Dark Invader grunted with ecstasy and nipped playfully at Sadiq's plump bottom. "Ari! Shaitan!" Sadiq cursed him happily and Ted saw, with another pang, that already they understood one another perfectly.

At a call from the Jemadar, the Quillan head man, imposing in his maroon-coloured turban, well-cut coat and small cane, the hand rubbing stopped and each man fitted his hands with leather pads, stuffed like boxing gloves, and began using them in a rhythm that resounded round the square: right pad, left pad hard on the horse, then both pads hit together in the air to free dust and sweat; thump, thump – thrump: thump, thump – thrump, over and over again for at least fifteen minutes while Ted stood as if mesmerised, watching. At last the rhythm ended, pads were put away, then came the final polishing with soft brushes and cloths; manes and tails were brushed out, tails bandaged into shape, hooves lifted and cleaned inside and out, then oiled. Finally the men stood by their horses as the Jemadar walked round. Sometimes he stopped, pointed with his cane, criticising sharply; sometimes he gave a nod of satisfaction. When he had made his inspection, he came up to John.

As John approved them, one by one, the horses were led out to walk round and round the track of tan for an hour's gentle exercise. This was the time when, in the cool of the evening, the owners, and sometimes jockeys and riding boys, gathered to watch, discuss, saunter on the grass or sit under the trees. Meanwhile the undergrooms prepared the feeds, each inspected by the Jemadar, cleaned and filled buckets of water, hung rugs and surcingles ready and made the bedding for the night, carefully edging it with the plait of straw Mother Morag had seen. Then they laid out the bed roll of their particular senior syce on his charpoy – a wooden-framed string bed – set on the verandah: "They *sleep* with their horses?" asked Ted.

"They pull their charpoys right across the stall," said John. "A good groom like Sadiq hardly lets his horse out of his sight all day."

To Ted it was as if, in more ways than one, he had stepped into a different world. It was not only the, to him, torrid air, the pale glare of the sky – the glare was dimming now as it fell towards evening; not only the strange smells and sounds, the brilliant colours in the garden of the boarding house. He had seen a whole hedge of poinsettias; their garish scarlet and upstanding stamens had startled him – they hardly seemed like flowers; nor did the crimson hibiscus bells, the beds of flaming cannas, and here, in the Quillan garden, the tumbled masses of bougainvil-laeas, the gorgeous blue of morning glory, paler blue of plumbago. Ted could not then put a name to any of these flowers, but he could to the parakeets, flying wild in the trees. It was not the shock of Scattergold Hall either, nor of Dahlia and the children, nor the surprise of the stables. Ted felt as though barriers that had penned him all his life had fallen down. After that sleep, when he had come out on the boarding house verandah, a travelling bearer had been waiting for him – 'bearer', he gathered, meant 'valet'. "I look after you, sahib. Save you much trouble. I, Anthony, have many good 'chits'" – which seemed to be references. "I look after you."

The fellow, with his smooth English, was almost in Ted's room and, "I look after meself," Ted had said gruffly, but the man had called him 'sahib', him, Ted, who, except for a few short seasons and the three years of the war, had always been a 'lad'. "Sahib!" Though they had only exchanged a few words, Ted felt free and more equal with John Quillan than he had ever done with Michael Traherne, for all their mutual affection and respect. When Michael had been a little boy, Ted had called him Master Michael and he had never sat down in the presence of Annette. Now, feeling happier than he had done since Michael had told him Dark Invader was sold, happier than he had thought he would ever be again, happier and somehow taller – "Such a little squirt of a man" people usually said of him – Ted stood with John Quillan, watching Sadiq and Ali at work.

Then he watched even more closely. It seemed to his experienced eye that now and again, especially when the strapping approached the Invader's neck, a muscle twitched and he flinched. At once Sadiq's hand discarded the leather pad to smooth and gentle the place and Dark Invader grunted with pleasure again but, "Might be," said Ted as he watched and, as he saw it repeated, "Might be – might do the trick." He thought he had said it under his breath, but John's sharp ears had heard.

Next day a big sandy-haired, soft-voiced man in breeches and Newmarket boots appeared with a sheaf of papers. This time John did introduce Ted: "Ted Mullins, Captain Mack, our Turf Club Official Vet. He has come, as you have probably guessed, to identify Dark Invader as the horse of that name and breeding entered in the Stud Book."

"Pleased to meet you," Ted said primly, but he watched anxiously as Captain Mack examined Dark Invader, checked his colouring and markings, looked at his teeth. Then he completed his notes and closed his book with a snap.

"What did he make of him, sir?" Ted asked John when the Captain had gone.

"Mack doesn't say much unless he's making a diagnosis. He said Dark Invader looked very like a horse."

Ted was visibly disappointed. "Was that all, sir?"

"Yes, Mullins."

That forbade any more questions but it was not all Captain Mack said. The same night he called round at Scattergold Hall for a drink and, when the bandar-log had got tired of their exuberant welcome and gone to their own occupations and Dahlia was singing the current baby to sleep, the two men sat comfortably drinking their whisky. Dahlia's slow lullaby punctuated their talk, the ayah's song that had lulled generations of foreign babies to sleep:

Nini, baba, nini,
Roti, mackan cheeni.
Sleep, baby, sleep,
Bread, butter and sugar.

"How I remember that," said Captain Mack. "I was out here as a child, you know," and his big body relaxed into peace.

Roti, mackan, cheeni . . .

"Don't go to sleep too," said John and called to the 'boy', as Dahlia persistently called him, but who was, in fact, John's Ooryah bearer, Danyal, to fill their glasses. It was not until after the fourth of the long pale whiskies, though, that Captain Mack said, "Leventine's new importation – that's one hell of a horse, John."

"So he may be, but he also has one hell of a record." John held out a paper. "Read this chit Mullins gave me from Michael Traherne."

Dear John,

I send you in the care of his lad, Ted Mullins, one of the nicest horses I have come across, which is saying a good deal.

From the viewpoint of our profession he is a problem. As you will see from his record, a win first time out in good company, nothing since; in fact the highlight of his three year old season was fifth in a field of washouts at Folkestone.

What the record does not show though is his form on the home gallops; at a mile and a half or upwards he is pretty nearly unbeatable – but *not* in public.

I had hoped to find the solution, but his owner

65

has lost patience, so . . . Now he's all yours and good luck to you.

"What do you make of that?" asked John.

Captain Mack pondered, then: "I don't like it. I don't like it one bit," he said. "It can't be a physical thing; if it were, it would be there all the time, home gallops or race. If we could find it we could probably cure it, but. . . ."

"You mean," said John, "a sound horse that won't try under pressure is usually one that has been whipped at the finish of a race and has learnt his lesson that if he takes the lead he will be punished."

"Exactly. 'The shadow of remembered pain.'" Sandy Mack was given to quotation. "It's in the mind, John. Besides, it's the leadership instinct; you don't need me to tell you, even in thoroughbreds, it's a rare and frail thing – crush it and it has gone for ever. No, John. I doubt if this hope of Leventine's will win any race this side of Doomsday."

"Any race! He's aiming at the Cups."

Captain Mack laughed. "What! The Viceroy's? I'm not a betting man and I won't bet with you, but if Dark Invader gets anywhere near that, I'll eat my hat."

"H'mmm," was all John said but, next evening, as he and Ted were watching the grooming down, "What did you mean, Mullins," he asked, "when you said this . . ." he gestured at the working grooms, "might do the trick?"

"You heard?" Ted was amazed.

"I heard. What did you mean?" Ted looked up at John. If a hawk or falcon could have blue eyes, thought John, this man's are like a hawk's, missing nothing, but Ted was silent. Some inward struggle was going on. John tried to help.

"Dark Invader was thoroughly vetted before he was bought, by the vet Mr. Leventine chose."

"He certainly was." The day after Michael's telephone call from Dilbury, a grizzled man in a bowler hat, brown gaiters and black boots had driven into the Traherne yard in a yellow-wheeled dog-cart drawn by a high-stepping hackney. "That was Major Woods, sir. He's well known and you should have seen the going over he gave the Invader. Even had his shoes off. Real old sort, that one," said Ted. "Did a proper job and time no object. Learned his trade before there were motor cars. He filled in a printed form with a mighty lot of words and told Mr. Michael: 'A.1. at Lloyds and sound as a bell of brass.' He knew a quality hoss when he saw one – meaning no disrespect to Captain Mack, of course."

"Well then," and John said quietly, "in spite of all that, and Captain Mack's opinion, you still think there's something wrong. What?"

"Ar!" Ted drew a breath of satisfaction. "Soon's I saw you, I knew one day you would be asking me that. I believe it's his muscles, sir, high on the shoulder."

"Yet they didn't find it?"

"Couldn't," said Ted. "Not looking at him like that. Can't see nothing, nor feel it. Pass your hand firm and there's nothing, but with pressure . . . muscles have two ends, sir, and it's deep. Did you see when Mr. Saddick . . ."

"Sadiq?"

"Yes. Mr. Saddick was strapping; the hoss flinched," and Ted burst out, "It was that Bacon what began it. Those damned bow legs of his. Nutcrackers," said Ted with venom. "Squeezing a hoss in a place God never meant a man's legs to be – he rides so short, see, and the Invader, he were nothing but a great sprawling baby, and it were his first race. But that Captain Hay was set on a win, no matter what."

"Which he got," said John.

"Yes." Ted's face was grim. "Will you watch, sir? Just watch – when Mr. Saddick lays it on hard."

John watched, standing close. In his presence, Sadiq and Ali doubled their efforts and, on the far side, as Sadiq came up the shoulder, John saw the Invader flinch and, "You're right," he told Ted. "There is a tender spot. We'll get Captain Mack to have a look."

Captain Mack stood, like John had, close beside the horse, but his scepticism showed as he let Ted, as far as Ted could reach, then Sadiq, guide his fingers slowly up the Invader's shoulder, pressing all the way. Suddenly the horse grew restive. "S-steady, Darkie, S-steady," hissed Sadiq, but Captain Mack pressed harder – scepticism had given way to intentness – harder, harder – there came a definite flinch and Dark Invader threw up his head, almost jerking Sadiq off his feet. "Ar!" whispered Ted as, "Get me something to stand on," ordered Captain Mack. "You great brute!" He clapped Dark Invader affectionately on his quarter. "You're tall as a giraffe," and, "That bench will do," he said and, as he got up, "Stand still, you," he said to Dark Invader as his fingers reached steadily on; a moment later he was looking with interest, not where Ted and Sadiq had shown him the tenderness, but above it, where the hairs of the mane came to an end and, "John," he said, "look here."

John joined him on the bench. "See anything?" asked the Captain. "Look. There's a scar under those white hairs."

"But . . . it's miniscule."

"On the surface. Mullins, hop up. Ever noticed that before?"

"Course," said Ted. "Them's the only other white hairs he's got. Had them when he come from Ireland. I reckon when he were a baby running loose he maybe caught a bit of barbed wire, or cut hisself – but that was long before, so it couldn't be the trouble . . . or could it?" Ted had seen Captain Mack's satisfaction. "*Could* it?"

"It could. In fact, I think that's it. Happened when he was a foal, guess you're right there, but not wire, rolling in the grass more like and met a bit of broken bottle or a sharp stone – anything – and made a small cut that healed on the surface but left damage; maybe a bit of gravel or a chip of glass got in and caused infection deeper down. The muscles lost flexibility – in fact grew fibrous – left a scar in the muscle if you like – nothing to see on the outside but any pressure on that spot would cause pain. When the horse was over-stretched, tired as well – remember how young he was . . ."

"It must have hurt like hell," said John, "and I can

guess that Streaky Bacon's grip just caught it, which could account for everything. Sandy, you clever old devil."

"Don't thank me, thank Ted and Sadiq." Captain Mack got down from the bench. "But you're not out of the wood yet. Sadiq's 'hart molesh' is the best possible treatment, but there's more to this than that. Everything to do with the finish of a race, other horses challenging, the noise, the excitement, tells Darkie, 'Stop before it hurts.' That's it, isn't it, old fellow," he pulled one of the dark ears.

"So we still have our problem."

"You do indeed. You now have to 'minister to a mind diseased'," and the Captain went on:

"'Pluck from the memory a rooted sorrow
Raze out the written troubles of the brain . . .'"

"*Macbeth* Act Five Scene III," said John, "so shut up and don't show off."

"Dear me!" said Captain Mack, "and I thinking that cavalry officers were semi-illiterate."

"Granted, but I acted in *Macbeth* at school. First Murderer."

"Pity you weren't the First Witch. You could do with a little magic just now."

"Meaning that you think it's still no go?"

"Meaning just that. John, face it. You know that a spoiled horse never comes back."

"Mullins," said John when Captain Mack had gone. "Why didn't you tell Mr. Traherne what you thought about the horse?"

Ted hesitated. "The Invader was never no trouble with me, sir, and there was nothing I could be sure of. I hoped Mr. Michael might see for hisself. Then when the hoss was sold, who was I," asked Ted, "to set meself up against a veterinary like Major Woods? Besides, if Mr. Michael had listened, it would have put him in a spot. Don't get me wrong, sir, Mr. Michael, or his father or his grandfather, come to that, would never have let a hoss be sold out of his stables if he didn't think it was sound, and Captain Hay . . " Ted spat, "he wouldn't have waited. If he had known, it would have been any old place for Dark Invader, maybe even the kick." Ted unashamedly drew his sleeve across his eyes and, for a moment, could not go on. "Mr. Michael couldn't have stopped that and I thought with Mr. Leven . . ."

"Leventine."

"Yes. You see, sir, two of them travelling lads would have done to bring out all his hosses to In'ja, but for the Invader he brought me out special so I thought with him . . ."

"Dark Invader might have a chance?"

"Yes sir, but has he? Couldn't follow all that talk," said Ted, "but I guess what the Captain meant was, if the Invader was to meet Streaky again, even now, he would remember."

"Possibly, but he won't see Streaky."

"Or his like?"

"Or his like. We'll see to that."

"Then – you think he has a chance in spite of Captain Mack?"

As always when John Quillan met opposition he

was obstinate and, "He's going to have a chance," said John.

"But how, sir?"

"I don't know how – yet – but somehow. We must see to it," and, "I'm glad you came, Ted."

"So am I," said Ted.

After dinner, when the last bandar had hushed, the last baby been fed, when Dahlia had gone to bed and the last round of the stables been done, John liked to light a cigar – he allowed himself one every evening – and then stroll among the tumbledown terraces and fountains of his scented garden to think over his plans and the problems of the day. Tonight it was Dark Invader.

John could visualise that first race at Lingfield. Dark Invader well away – Michael Traherne had assured him the horse was a willing starter – but when the field caught up with him, forced to quicken his stride by an almighty squeeze in an unexpected place and John saw the typical Bacon finish, the furiously urgent figure, the rhythmically swinging whip, shown but not striking, the horse desperately extended, those legs, thighs and knees gripping vice-like above the flimsy saddle. It must have hurt hideously – "a stab from a knife", Mack had said. Poor old Darkie, thought John. That's probably what you were trying to tell us stupid old human blockheads. Well, we're there at last, but what to do about it? What the hell to do about it, I don't know. With which dispiriting thought he threw away the butt of his cigar, called to

Gog and Magog and turned to go to bed.

On the verandah he paused; certain troubled, puzzled and honest phrases were coming back to him. "I never had no trouble with him . . .", "Had it when he come over from Ireland . . . but that was before . . .", "I never had no trouble with him," and, "I wonder," said John to Gog and Magog, "I wonder."

"Ted," said John next morning – Mullins had now permanently become Ted – "I have been doing some thinking. I should like you to show me how you ride Dark Invader. Will you?"

"Will I?" It was Dark Invader's fourth day in India and during early work John had had him walked quietly down to the racecourse and on to the exercise track. "Will I? Thought I would never be on him again," said Ted.

Like most trainers, John Quillan retained his own jockey, a young quarter English, three quarters Chinese, whose name was Ah Lee, but whom everybody called Ching. Ted had already met him, lithe, slim, eager, his black eyes alert. John had picked him out from a set of young jockeys from Singapore and had slowly trained him. Now, "Will Mr. Ching mind?" asked Ted. "It's the Invader's first ride here."

"No. No. I like to see, maybe learn," but Ching was obviously puzzled as he stood with John, watching.

Dark Invader had acknowledged Ted's arrival in the saddle with a backward slant of an ear. Nothing else. "Not much awkwardness about him after a month at sea," said John.

73

"I didn't expect it, sir. Easiest horse alive," and Ted told Dark Invader, "Walk on, boy. *That*'s the fella! Just a little trot now. Gently does it," and Dark Invader trotted round the circuit soberly, as he was told. There were new things to look at: a fat little sheep: three geese: rough-bottomed baskets full of horse dung: a vulture picking at some small dead animal. Dark Invader examined them all with prick-eared attention, without faltering in his steady trotting. Then, "That's enough," Ted seemed to say as he brought the big horse round and back to where Sadiq was waiting. Ted slipped to the ground and patted the handsome neck, while Dark Invader nosed impatiently at his pockets.

"Thanks, Ted." John came up. "Just what was wanted." Then, "Ted, would you ride a bit of work for me? Would you take Snowball, that old grey there, and do the whole circuit with the riding boy on that bay mare? She's to race in a fortnight's time. Snowy's not in the same class, but he has been racing in the Monsoon Meeting so he's that much fitter. Take them along to the four furlong mark and come home as fast as you like."

"Fast! On Snowy!" said Ching.

"Exactly. The mare should lose him fairly quickly," said John.

Snowball's stud book name was Arctic Elegance; he was Australian bred, a gelding, now twelve years old; his coat, once grey, had whitened, his teeth yellowed and the hollows over his eyes sunk deeper. Years of slogging round the same racing and practice course had hardened his mouth and soured his temper. "I

74

hate ride him," said Ching.

John watched closely as Ted began by taking the old horse round and round their group, and saw how Snowball tried to get his snaffle-bit into its usual position against his back teeth – and failed to get it to stay there. "Hands!" said John to Ching. "Watch Mullins's hands." They saw Snowball begin to chase the bit with his tongue with a flicker of interest. Then John heard Ted's voice, "Cheer up, old cuddy. 'Tisn't such a bad old world," and saw him run a finger up the side of the hogged mane and pull one of the stiff ears in what seemed one continuous movement. Snowball shook himself and gave a little hoist to his quarters. "Good boy," said Ted. "Come on, let's show them what we old 'uns can do," as they set off to join the mare and riding boy. "The touch of the craftsman," said John, but Ching did not understand. At the four furlong mark, John pressed his stop watch and waited for the mare to draw away from Snowball. After a furlong she led by half a length but could not shake him off, and Snowball finished galloping stride for stride with his head level with her girth. The stop watch showed a satisfactory time for the mare, a surprising one for Snowball. "Well, well," said John. "The old English long rein finish. I never thought to see it in this city."

Ching was almost too dumbfounded to speak. At last, "Is English style?" he asked incredulously.

"Was," said John. He walked over to where the riders had trotted back, noting with increased respect Ted's steady hand and unhurried breathing. They dismounted and John said again, "Thank you, Ted. You certainly sweetened that old plug and kept him going. He didn't even do his usual ducking out towards the rubbing-down sheds."

"No, I told him different." Ted said it as if it were every day – as it is with him, thought John. "I think I often know what's in a hoss's mind before he knows hisself. Comes from being with them."

With them in more senses than one, thought John, but, aloud, "I can guess that's true." Then he said directly, "Ridden with the best in your day, haven't you, Ted?"

"I did quite a lot," Ted admitted. "Pre-war Derby, four times. Never in the frame, though. Come to think of it, I was third in the Oaks once, and fifth twice."

"And what are you doing now when not seeing the world free of charge?" They were walking towards the Stands. "Still riding?"

"No . . . retired from all that."

John heard a pause. Lost his ticket, he thought. I wonder why.

"Didn't do much after the war," Ted went on. "It didn't seem to matter. You see, I lost my wife in the 'flu epidemic – '18 that was."

"I'm sorry."

"Her name was Ella." John did not know it, but this was a rare confidence; Ted had not spoken Ella's name in all these years. "Wouldn't swop my Ted for the King of England." Ella had often said that; she had made Ted feel like the King of England too. Ella, a heap of clay with his flowers beaten into the soil by the rain, and yet it seemed to Ted now as if Ella were suddenly with him again, Egging me on to talk,

76

thought Ted. "Mr. Michael, he took me on 'cos of his father, I think. A man on his own doesn't need much," said Ted. "So I did my two, same as when I was a nipper. Must admit there was a bit of whisky – more'n a bit. Then the Invader came – from Ireland it was. I remember the day. After that it was just him. Somehow I never got round to thinking he would be sold. . . . Now . . ." and Ted looked away over the green distances of the Maidan, then quickly recollected himself. "'Spect I'll make out," and, "You were saying, sir?"

"I was interested in your finish, the long rein," said John. "Seems a lost art. The boys nowadays can't drive a horse without climbing up its neck and think they're not on the job unless they're chewing its ears off. Interesting too that you don't ride as short as most."

"Not surprising. When I were a boy, it was all straight legs, toes down. Soon we was all taught different, but I never took to the very short style, like Streaky's – legs doubled up like a frog."

"Yes. I should guess you ride four to six holes longer," and John again said thoughtfully, "I wonder."

Ted had a fortnight before his ship, the *City of Benares* this time, sailed for England and, "You should see something of India," John told him. "You could easily make a tour, go to Darjeeling and see the Snows. Everest."

"They are lovelee," said Dahlia. She and Ted were now fast friends.

"Delhi, Agra and the Taj Mahal," said John.

"They are lovelee too."

"And you could go across and see the Ellora and Ajunta caves and sail from Bombay," but all of India Ted wanted to see was here in the Quillan stables – the track that led down to the racecourse, the racecourse itself and its circuits. "Well, what do you want to do?"

Ted cleared his throat. "If it's all right by you, sir, could I stay here a little longer? There's another boat in about three weeks' time, and I think Mr. Michael could spare me as he hasn't the Invader; and as I'm here . . . I have a bit put by so could pay my way."

"No need for that," said John. "I was wishing you could give me a hand. Ching hasn't much experience. There's Dark Invader to acclimatise and," he added as an afterthought, "Mr. Leventine."

Back from Europe Mr. Leventine came to watch the evening parade. Several owners were there, sitting on the seats or benches, walking, gossiping and visiting their horses, giving them sugar-cane, carrots, even apples. "Apples! Probably from Kulu! Think what they cost!" Sister Ignatius would have said. The owners patted necks and pulled ears affectionately, talked to the grooms, often consulted with John, sometimes Ching or the Jemadar. Never at this time was there a sign of Dahlia or the bandar-log.

Gog and Magog, sitting on each side of the verandah steps, kept guard – no owners' dogs dared intrude. Ayahs were putting the babies to bed, the

children were having their supper. Now and again a
wail or the sound of a child fight would float out over
the lawn, but this was one rule that had to be kept
because, "Out of sight, out of mind – almost," John
said bitterly. It took time for Ted to understand.

Mr. Leventine's arrival was different from anyone
else's, as was his car, a large Minerva, painted deep
blue with huge brass lamps and a bulb horn in the
shape of a brass serpent. The chauffeur was in blue
to match, with polished brass buttons, and another
servant with a crested turban sat beside him; his duty
was to open doors and carry any possessions Mr.
Leventine happened to have with him. Mr. Leventine
himself was in a pale grey suit, a carefully folded white
silk handkerchief in the breast pocket, a pink rose in
his buttonhole. He also wore brown and white laced
shoes, the sort unkindly called 'co-respondent', of
which he was innocently unaware. Of the other
owners, the men, mostly in jerseys, sports coats and
flannels, looked dusty and shabby beside him and as
he advanced with a strong waft of cologne, a few said,
"Good evening, Leventine," but most of them parted
before him and became immersed in talk. Only Lady
Mehta smiled and waved.

"Well, Johnny. How are you?" and Mr. Leventine
laid a diamond-ringed hand on John's shoulder who
was spared from responding, "And you, Cas?" as Mr.
Leventine would have liked him to, because the
excited voice went straight on: "Where are they?" Mr.
Leventine had not come to meet people, but to look at
his horses. "Where is he?"

"Dark Invader?"

"Of course."

John presented Ted who was given a curt nod. Ted could see nothing wrong with Mr. Leventine. "Dressed up," he would have conceded that, "but that's natural, isn't it? He's some sort of foreigner and they have different ways. Can guess he's very rich, probably doesn't know how rich he is, but not half as much a show-off as Captain Hay. Talks loud 'cos he's interested," and Ted followed as Mr. Leventine went along the stables – his horses had been kept in for his visit – discussing each with John. Then they came to Dark Invader who whickered when he saw Ted.

"Ah!" said Mr. Leventine and stood still. Ted noticed that Sadiq's eyes gleamed at the sight of Mr. Leventine and he gave a deep salaam. "Ah!" and then, "You asked me why I bought him," said Mr. Leventine in a reverent tone. "Well, look, Johnny. Look." Mr. Leventine's voice was as loud as if he were addressing a stadium. "Look at him. He's bred to the big Open races." Then he lowered his voice. "I can guess what happened. His owner – this Captain Hay – is, by all accounts, a young man, ambitious for a big win, not interested in anything else. They tried Dark Invader, a certainty to win first time out as a two year old, got good odds about him ante post and engaged the famous Tom Bacon to ride him. Colt was green; got left six lengths but Bacon had his orders so he set about him and got him home."

"Correct," whispered Ted under his breath.

"Colt hasn't tried a yard since. Why? He's bred right, looks right and moves right."

"Hear, hear," whispered Ted.

"But isn't right," John said it calmly.

"Then find out why," commanded Mr. Leventine. Then he dropped his voice still further. "Don't you see, now's our chance, Johnny. His record's so terrible he'll be put in Class IV with a lot of Australian washouts and English weeds, and so . . . slowly, slowly, if we handle him carefully, he need never have another hard race."

"Till he gets back to his own class."

Mr. Leventine gave his trainer a long, purposeful stare. "He's in a class by himself," said Mr. Leventine with finality.

"That's what I say." Ted was suddenly bold enough to speak aloud, and Mr. Leventine turned. "Johnny said you were. . . ?"

"Ted Mullins, sir."

"Ah! I remember. The Dark Invader's stable lad." Mr. Leventine, Ted noted, did not call him Darkie. "The one I had come out with him."

"That's right," said Ted, "and I thank you, sir."

The unexpectedly good manners – "It was Ella kept me up to that" – struck even Mr. Leventine. He gave Ted an even longer, harder look than he had given John, then made what John called 'one of the swift and, usually irrevocable, Leventine decisions.' "Johnny," he said, "this man must stay with the horse."

"Stay?"

"Right through," said Mr. Leventine.

"But he's working for Michael Traherne," began John and, "perhaps Traherne can't spare him . . ."

"Traherne," and the, for Ted, omnipotent Michael

was brushed away like a fly. "Settle terms, any terms they like," ordered Mr. Leventine, "but this man must stay."

Against his usual custom – he detested getting up early – Mr. Leventine began to come down for the morning's work, wrapped in a camelhair coat, his throat muffled in a cashmere scarf. His footman or car attendant or bearer, "or what-you-call-him," said John, stood behind him holding a shooting stick, a handsome pair of binoculars, and a topee for when the sun grew warm. Mr. Leventine watched with John as Ching on chosen horses, the riding boys on others, and Ted on Dark Invader, took their turn.

The scene was always the same; each trainer had his 'camp' with horses and syces moving round it, a heap of rugs and saddlery in the middle. The Jemadar called the horses out to the group of waiting riders; John watched tensely, sometimes worried, sometimes delighted. Sometimes he mounted Matilda to ride further up the circuit; sometimes he went on foot, but always shadowed, though never intruded upon, by Gog and Magog, the amber of their paws and flanks wet and dark with dew.

After work, while the grooms and riding boys walked the horses home, most trainers and their owners and jockeys went over to the stands for coffee and chat. John avoided this, riding Matilda straight back to the stables, but with Mr. Leventine it was different; he demanded his full rights and talking about his horses, the daily discussion, was one of these.

Over coffee he asked suddenly, "Why isn't that little man riding for Micky?" – it was the first time John had heard anyone call Michael Traherne 'Micky'. John had told Mr. Leventine about Ted's riding of Snowball, Arctic Elegance; at the time Mr. Leventine had only said, "Humph!" but he had watched Ted minutely and, "That man's a jockey," said Mr. Leventine firmly.

"Yes. He was quite well known before the war."

"Then why?"

"Lost his licence."

"Not mixed up in any dirty work, I hope." The small brown eyes were sharp.

"Wouldn't be with Traherne if he had," said John. "It was a doping case. Mullins obviously didn't know anything about it but, as you know, once the powers get working they'll warn off anything in sight up to and including the stable cat, and ask questions afterwards. Poor Ted!"

"Humph!" said Mr. Leventine.

"More coffee?" John had to ask it twice, but Mr. Leventine said neither "yes" nor "no". He beckoned to his henchman and was gone.

In the evenings, after his visit to the stables, Mr. Leventine liked to play billiards at the Turf Club. The Royal Calcutta Turf Club was the only Club where he was an acceptable member; its criteria were not colour, race or class, but a true interest in racing and absolute integrity, points on which no-one could have failed Casimir Alaric Bruce Leventine. He was more than proud of his membership, loving the Club's spacious flower-filled park, its airy rooms, the prestige of its portraits of past Senior Stewards, and admiring its members with most of whom he could not have fraternised except through racing and games like billiards. On this particular evening, it was by a lucky chance that, in a tournament, he was playing against one of the most eminent, the High Court Judge Sir Humphrey Hyde, who was also a Steward and, "one of Calcutta's monuments in the world of racing," John Quillan would have said.

The game was a close one and, though Mr. Leventine was good – indeed, was known to have a surprising virtuosity – he lost by a narrow margin. Sir Humphrey, who did not mind winning, was amused by the ingenuity with which Mr. Leventine allowed it. "I wondered what the fellow wanted," he told a crony afterwards. "Favour from the Bench? Hardly, he's too shrewd and far too well established. Racing? Probably. I suspect he wants to be a Steward. Well, in a year or two's time, why not?" but that, for once, was not in Mr. Leventine's mind. "I have a new horse," he said.

"Several," said the Judge. "I have been looking at the new arrivals you have just registered. One of them puzzled me. Dark Invader – is that the one?" Mr. Leventine nodded. "More fashionably bred than we usually see here," said Sir Humphrey. "Indian stake money doesn't as a rule justify the price you must have paid."

"I got him cheaply," said Mr. Leventine. "Spoiled by a hard race as a two year old. I'm hoping he'll change his ways."

"Rogues don't as a rule."

"Perhaps he won't, but he's not a rogue; besides . . ."

"Besides?"

"I don't like to see such beauty and breeding
thrown on the scrap-heap."

"You're a good chap, Leventine," the Judge did
not say it aloud, but his look of approval said it for him
and, for the first time, for anyone in that Club, he gave
Mr. Leventine a pat on the shoulder. "I wish you luck
with him."

"Thank you, Sir Humphrey," said Mr. Leventine
with just the right touch of deference. "I expect I'll
need it." He did not say any more that night.

Ted fitted quickly and happily into the life of the
Quillan stable and, to his own surprise, into Scattergold Hall. John had suggested he move from the
boarding house into a one-roomed annex among the
many at the Hall. Ted's scrupulous soul was satisfied
when John let him pay his rent and board from the
salary – to Ted enormous – that Mr. Leventine paid
him. Michael had agreed without demur to his
staying – "I can't imagine anything happier for Ted,"
he had told Annette – so that there was no disloyalty.
Ted liked his stone-floored room; its windows and
doorways had shutters, no glass or door – in the day-
time a curtain hung across the doorway; the furniture
was so plain that his scant possessions did not seem
too cheap, yet there were things he had never had
before – and appreciated – a bathroom of his own

and a private verandah with cane chairs and a table; along the verandah edge the gardeners put pots of violets and carnations. "I didn't think vi'lets grew in In'ja."

The bearer, Danyal, looked after Ted's clothes, made his bed and dusted his room, "But you mustn't ask him to touch any food," said John. "It's against his caste." It was Ahmed, a Muslim, who brought Ted his meals from the kitchen. The sweeper, called Khokhil, a handsome, tall man, but an Untouchable, swept the floors and cleaned the bathroom, "except the basin," said John, "or the drinking and tooth glasses – he mustn't touch them. They are Danyal's province." Another of Khokhil's permitted functions was to look after the dogs and he was as proud of Gog and Magog as Ted was of Dark Invader – but an Untouchable! Ted shrank from the idea of that; indeed, it all seemed topsy-turvy to him. "What would Ella say?" and he was sometimes embarrassed. Ahmed had wanted to stand behind Ted's chair while he ate, but Ted begged John to tell Ahmed to leave the dishes and go away. John did tell Ahmed but, "You will have to get used to it, Ted," he said. "In a way it's a sort of respect – not for us but from us."

"You mean we recognise their ways." That made Ted feel easier – he was used to giving respect, not to getting it – and soon he fell into the routine, almost the rhythm of the day. It began with the rise at dawn, a tray of tea and, to Ted, extraordinary, buttered toast and bananas brought to him by Ahmed, who seemed to work at all hours and never, Ted was to discover, had a day off or a holiday. Then came the ride down to

86

the racecourse – Dark Invader coming behind as he had done at Dilbury – and the morning's work, carefully regulated by John to the demands of the Invader's big frame with long periods of walking or trotting under Ted's expert hands. After that the slow walk back, when Ted had, perforce, to watch Sadiq and Ali do the rubbing down, grooming and the morning feed. "As Mr. Leventine's paying me, couldn't I, sir?"

"These are my stables and my syces," John reminded him.

"Sorry, sir."

"Besides, it's not the custom," John said more gently, "and in India we don't go against that."

After breakfast, an English breakfast, came the cleaning of the tack, saddles, bridles, reins, stirrup-leathers; stirrups, bits and whips had to be laid out for inspection. This was the time, too, when Captain Mack came; he was called for the slightest cause. "We don't take chances with other people's horses," said John.

At two o'clock, when the midday feed was done and the men themselves had gone by turn to cook and eat, for horses and syces alike came peace – the syces asleep on their charpoys, the beasts in their stalls. Then, the only sound in the stables was a human snore or the stamp of a hoof or swish of a tail to keep the flies away – the horses wore light nets that even covered neck and heads. A crow might give a lazy caw, a goose or duck quack, hens scratch, but the cats were curled in the verandah chairs, the Great Danes stretched prone on the floor. John slept too, as did Dahlia and the babies, even the children, though not as long as the servants, and the gateman retired into his little cell by the gate, "for a whole two hours!" said Ted.

At first he had tried to keep awake. "Sleep in the afternoon!" but the general laziness caught him too, or perhaps it was the after effect of the curry and rice he was beginning to like, and that Dahlia ordered every day; it was only the rattle of china that woke him when Ahmed again brought tea and Ted heard the Jemadar's call in the stables, the horses' answering neighs, and it was time for more work; sometimes back to the racecourse for an hour, sometimes schooling in the school yard, then the evening ritual.

Dark Invader had taken to the country as though in some previous incarnation he had been an inhabitant. He made no objection to the villainous crows that sidled along the bars of the open stall and robbed his food tub. He blew appreciatively on the huge ram that lived in the yard, and formed a grave and kindly friendship with the bandar-log and accepted their offerings of stolen sugar and sweetmeats out of the bazaar: jilipis, sticky sugar rings dripping with sweetness, coconut ice or sandesh – thick white toffee. Above all he liked the attention. "He must have been a Maharajah," said John. "A pasha with slaves." His muscles began to harden, his coat to glow. His appetite was prodigious.

The fact that Dark Invader's food cost three times Sadiq's total pay, four times Ali's, did not worry them at all. By the standard of their trade they were well off and had prestigious and steady work at Quillan's where each was given a blanket, a thick coat of serge, a brown woollen jersey for the winter and two cotton shirts for summer, and was allowed to wear a conical skull-cap with a soft cloth turban wound round it in the Quillan maroon. Sadiq lived and slept on the verandah in front of his horse's box. Twice a day he handed over for an hour to Ali while he went to cook and eat his food, and five times a day he turned his face towards Mecca and, as a good Muslim, made his prayers, standing, bowing, kneeling, touching his forehead to the ground as he muttered them. Ali, when Sadiq came back, did the same.

Sadiq was a happy man but, "Eighteen rupees a month!" Ted exploded. "That's less than seven shillings a week!" It was enough for Sadiq; food for the month cost six rupees, twelve annas, so that ten, sometimes eleven rupees would be sent by money order each month to his family; once a year he took a month's leave and travelled to Bihar to see them. "That's a rum go," said Ted, trying to think of himself parted from Ella for eleven months of the year and, what was more, "I think this year I no go," said Sadiq.

"But you *must*. You wife, children . . ." but, "Not go," said Sadiq and smoothed Dark Invader's mane. "I stay him."

The co-operation between the two – necessary, Ted had to admit – was complete; the horse's great handsome head would come down to be groomed, to have the head-collar put on, to accept the bridle. He had never been as confident and tractable. With Ted to ride him, Sadiq always near, and the wonderful 'hart molesh' that was beginning to disperse that spot

of tenderness, pain and fear seemed to have vanished.
"Come on a marvel," Ted wrote to Michael Traherne.
"But he hasn't raced yet," said John.

IV

For four months of the year Bengal's cold weather, or winter, is halcyon, "for those with warm clothes," said Sister Ignatius. As November turned to December, when the string went down in the morning, mists swirled round the horses' legs and lay so thick over the Maidan that John had difficulty tracking the course through his binoculars. By the time the horses had finished the evening parade, it was dusk, the brief Indian twilight called by the Bengalis, 'cow-dust time', because it was then that the cattle were driven home; almost at once the light faded, it was night and all along the stalls hand lanterns were lit; though there was electricity, the syces needed the lanterns to look at hooves, and deep into the food tubs to see how much of the feed had been eaten or left. The horses were warmly rugged, then bedded down for the night. John issued extra blankets for the men.

He also sent a warm achkan, a long coat, to the Convent for Gulab. "We are issuing new ones for the men and I thought you could use this." He sent too a horse rug for Solomon. "You needn't thank me. It's patched," "Patched or not, it is a Godsend," wrote Mother Morag. The Sisters wore their long black cloaks and hoods made of sturdy French frieze when

91

they went 'collecting', and for early prayer and Mass. "But I hardly like to wear mine," said Sister Mary Fanny, "when I think of the thousands . . ."

"Well, you're not going to do them any good if you get bronchitis," said Sister Ignatius, and Mother Morag intervened, "To help people, Sister, you must keep reasonably well yourself," but she knew only too well what little defence a cotton shirt or a thin muslin sari or a toddler's tiny jacket that only came just past the navel was against the chill and, for the 'poorest of the poor', she wondered which was worst – the heat or the deluges and dankness of the monsoon or the cold? But at least, for most, the sun was no longer an enemy; humans and beasts alike could bask in it at midday and in the afternoons; its light had a soft golden quality that enhanced the colours in everything from the scarlet and gold of the Viceroy's Bodyguard to the delicate shades of the imported English annuals that flowered in the gardens of the – by Convent and Indian standards – rich. "Never thought to see sweet peas in In'ja," Ted said, as he had said of the violets.

It was a time of mixed flowers: in Calcutta's China-town narcissi were sold in Chinese porcelain bowls filled with gravel and chippings; in the gardens, with roses, petunias and pinks, the tropical flowers Ted had marvelled at still bloomed and there were new ones: the pink and white sandwich creeper that festooned walls and gateways and on the stable's lawn frangipani trees blossomed into their strange temple flowers that looked almost chiselled in the thickness of their petals, growing without leaves directly on bare thickened branches. Ted had never smelled anything like the headiness of their fragrance.

Unknown to him, Calcutta's 'season' was in full swing. Though no longer the capital of India, it was still a city of importance with its own Governor, the Governor of Bengal, but in December and early January the Viceroy came from Delhi and the old Palace of Belvedere, with all the splendour of its marble terraces, sweeps of steps, its state rooms and park, was opened. On state occasions both sets of Excellencies drove out in four-horse landaus with postillions and an escort of Bodyguards. The roads were spread with sand to make the tarmac less slippery for the horses, so the gorgeous equipages whirled along almost soundlessly, leaving a memory of brilliant uniforms and glittering metal and a cloud of dust which, every year, brought an epidemic of 'Calcutta' sore throats.

It was now that the most important races were run, including the Viceroy's cup on Boxing Day. The All India Polo Tournament and the Golf Championships were held, and there were Balls, both at Belvedere and Government House; invitations were vied for. There were private Balls too: the Vingt-et-Un given by twenty-one of Calcutta's promising young bachelors and the even more exclusive Unceremonials, the Senior or Burra-Sahib's Ball. Invitations to these could not be vied for; guests were asked – or not asked.

It was a lively time – for a few. Wives and daughters arrived from England, Scotland, Europe or the hills. The men's English suits and dress clothes were brought out from the airtight tin boxes where they had been stored to be safe from white ants and the mildew of the monsoon; though hung out in the sun, the lounge and morning suits, dinner jackets and 'tails' still gave out the scent of mothballs.

There were dinners, brunches on Sunday mornings after riding; often four or five cocktail parties had to be attended on the same night.

All this concerned John only over the racing. He could not bring himself to watch the polo. "Watch! You should be playing," protested Bunny. "You're a six handicap man, for heaven's sake!" John did not answer and, "You would be welcome, John." Bunny was watching his friend's face. "No, thank you, Bunny," and Bunny sighed.

Mother Morag was concerned because the canisters were filled to overflowing; in fact, they had to take extra ones because restaurants and hotels were crowded. "It's welcome, of course, our people need it in colder weather," but she worried in case the extra load were too much for Solomon.

It concerned Ted and Dark Invader not at all. They stayed in their own world of the stables, racecourse and the track on the verge of Lower Circular Road that lay between them; among the natives they mixed only with the Sadiqs, Alis, Ahmeds and Khokhils who attended to their wants – Ted still persisted with Mr. Saddick, Mr. Ally, Mr. Ar-med, Mr. Cockle. He was invariably kind to Mr. Ching and Sir Jemadar and the riding boys. Only once did Dahlia tempt him into the city, and that was to buy a gauzy Indian scarf, patterned in gold for Annette Traherne, and a length of tussore silk to make Michael a summer coat,

Christmas presents sent home by one of the travelling lads on the boat he should have caught. "Ted never forgets anyone," said John.

"What *has* happened to the children?" Mother Morag asked John when, as had become a habit, on Sunday mornings, he fetched them and Dahlia from Mass. "What *has* happened?"

"A little Englishman called Ted Mullins," said John.

Mother Morag had picked out Dark Invader at once from her window and noticed he was ridden by a small white man; noted, too, his stillness in the saddle compared to the riding boys, and his quiet authority when the big horse cocked his ears in curiosity or tried to swerve or break out of his walk and, thinking of that, she said, "What works with animals, works with children too."

Ted had been scandalised by the bandar-log. "I never did," he could not help saying to John.

"I know." John sounded helpless – and sad, thought Ted. "Nobody seems to be able to do anything with them. Mrs. Quillan's wonderful with babies, but . . ."

Ted cleared his throat. "Seeing how with Mr. Saddick and Mr. Ally I've so little to do for the hoss . . ."

"You would like to try your hand on my monkeys?"

"Well, sir, my wife was a school-teacher – miles above me, she was. She taught me – lots. So . . . if you and Mrs. Quillan wouldn't mind."

"*Mind!* We would be infinitely obliged but I doubt if you can even catch them."

Ted did not say he had caught them already.

They had been attracted first by Dark Invader. "We have never had a horse like that" – Ted noticed the 'we'. Now and again he swung one of them up on the Invader's back, but that was a privilege and Ted knew how to bestow his privileges. Then came a mutual respect for each other's riding; they had come to echo their father's reverence for Ted, and Ted had watched them schooling. Certainly know their business, he thought, but off the ponies! "Turned nine and ten and don't know your tables! Seven and you don't know your alphabet! Disgraceful!" he told them and, as with Dark Invader and countless other horses, the stricter he was with them, the more they adored him. "Now stand up and begin: twice five are ten: three fives are fifteen." "CAT: RAT: BAT . . . Go on. You can read that easy."

"You're sure they don't come for nuts and bananas?" said John.

"Nuts and bananas!" Ted said scornfully. "That's just about what they had, begging your pardon, sir," and, "Stand up. Keep still. This is a hanky, see. You blow your nose on *it*, not on your fingers. Disgusting!"

It had culminated on a Sunday morning when he had met Dahlia on the drive, wearing a linen suit, stockings, high-heeled shoes and a hat; she was carrying a bag, parasol and gloves and was accompanied by the children dressed as their usual selves.

"Where are you going?"

"To church." Dahlia gave him her happy smile. "I am taking the children, m'n."

"Taking the children like *that!*" Long ago memories of Sunday School came up in Ted; Sunday School, clean collars, being scrubbed even behind his ears, his nails inspected, and he was shocked. "To church like that!"

"I do try," wailed Dahlia. "Their clothes are all laid out. Clean shirts and shorts and frocks. They have them all, my God, *and* clean socks and shoes, but they won't . . ."

"Won't they!" To Ted, this was something far more important than the respect due to John and Dahlia as his superiors, to John's expertise as a trainer. What would Ella have done? and, "I'll give you ten minutes," he said to the bandar-log. "Wash faces and hands and knees, clean nails. Brush hair. Change into your clean clothes, be neat and tidy and come back ready, and I *mean* ready," said Ted.

John took Ted to the races; the Quillan stable had more than thirty runners that season, "So I'm here on business," said John. "Not as one of your groomed-up apes." Ted thought the 'grooming-up' very pretty, "like Ascot, it is," he said, but it brought him another pang. When Dark Invader won here, and Ted was sure he would, it was Sadiq who would lead him round the paddock, Sadiq who would attend him and Mr. Leventine when Mr. Leventine led him in. He, Ted, would have no part in it except to watch as he was watching now. John kept to the paddocks, the rubbing down sheds and the reserved stand which trainers and jockeys frequented. He accepted no invitations for iced coffee or tea. He had reason to be sour; Lady Mehta's Flashlight running in the Viceroy's Cup, was not even placed.

"Never mind, Johnny," said Mr. Leventine.

"I do mind," said John shortly, "and I mind for Lady Mehta."

"She should never have bought Flashlight," Mr. Leventine seemed basking in some warm secret thoughts of his own. He had no need to shake out his suits from airtight boxes, they travelled with him to Europe, or he bought new ones. Now he was impeccable in his usual pale grey from head to foot. "Like one of our state elephants," said Bunny. "He only needs some ornaments and tassels," but Mr. Leventine had no need of tassels; with his rose in his buttonhole, he was perfectly contented.

Every morning too he braved the mist and appeared, the Minerva dropping him at the stands, from which he walked, "actually walked!" said John, to join him, then stood, his binoculars trained on the striding figure of Dark Invader and the dot on his back that was Ted.

Mr. Leventine had an appointment with Sir Humphrey Hyde in his Chambers. Sir Humphrey was not surprised – "I had guessed he wanted something." Now he leaned forward, his elbows on his desk, his finger tips joined – he was a mannered judge – and said, "Well?"

THE DARK HORSE

The room with its littered table, bookcases filled with heavy, leather-bound books, its austere look, not of an office, but of a study of a particularly learned style, subdued Mr. Leventine and, "It's good of Your Honour to see me," he began.

"Not at all. I'm here to see people,'' and the Judge said gently, "Sir Humphrey would be in order." Then, "I gather we are not on legal business."

"No Sir . . . Humphrey. It's a racing matter. Matter of a jockey who is here – name of Mullins. As I understand it, he had ridden a lot in England but now he has no licence, and I wondered if it would be possible to find out, on the quiet, how he really came to lose it – I have heard one side of the story and it seems he was blameless – and whether there would be any bar to his riding here?"

"I could do that easily," said Sir Humphrey. "One of the Jockey Club Stipendaries is an old friend of mine. I could send him a cable, but tell me about this man – Mullins, did you say? What is so special about him?"

"You remember the new horse we spoke about in the Club the other night? Mullins came out with the shipment. He tells me he was Dark Invader's groom at Lingfield and the other races."

"Ah! Dark Invader, the well-bred horse with the slightly questionable racing record."

"Mullins swears the horse is genuine at bottom. Only needs to be ridden in a style that doesn't frighten him."

There was a pause. Sir Humphrey was obviously searching the filing cabinets of his legally trained memory. Then, "Diamond Jubilee," he said. "His lad rode him in all his races."

"Exactly." Mr. Leventine positively sparkled. "Diamond Jubilee, the King's horse. Wouldn't have that leading jockey, Mornington Cannon, at any price. Actually savaged him but, when they put up his lad, Jones, he won every race. The Two Thousand, St. Leger, Derby, everything."

"I think I remember Mullins. Ted Mullins, wasn't it?" Sir Humphrey leaned back in his swivel chair. "If your Mullins and mine are the same, I owe him a good turn. I often had a bet on him when I was a young barrister and the nimble shilling was hard to come by."

Mr. Leventine smiled dutifully. He had no idea what a nimble shilling was, but it seemed Sir Humphrey was favourably inclined. Mr. Leventine, though, thought it still necessary to press the point. "The important thing, Your Honour, I mean, Sir Humphrey, is to find out if he can race here."

"That I have understood." Mr. Leventine was not sure if that was a rebuke or a reassurance. "I'll find out for you with pleasure."

Mr. Leventine had to wait ten days, and Sir Humphrey did not summon him to his Chambers; they met, it seemed by chance, in the billiard room at the Club, but it was Sir Humphrey who challenged Mr. Leventine to a game. It was not until they had finished and Sir Humphrey was carefully putting his cue away in the black japanned tube that carried his name in white letters that he said, "By the way, Leventine, good news. Your man is all right. Nothing against him. Could have had his licence back long ago but didn't apply."

"So he could have a licence now?"

"Certainly. He has only to apply with the necessary backing."

"We shall, but of course we shan't be ready till next cold weather."

"Well, don't go telling me any stable secrets," Sir Humphrey laughed, "and Ted Mullins *is* my man. Give him my compliments and tell him he used to carry my money twenty years ago."

Mr. Leventine ordered the Minerva and drove straight to Scattergold Hall to see John Quillan.

"You mean I can ride again?" asked Ted.

India is a land of timelessness and time had slipped past for Ted, immersed in his work with Dark Invader and the children.

The cold weather ended. February began to grow warm and Calcutta's glory of flowering trees, the scarlet flowers of the silk cotton trees, the riot of orange and red of the gol-mohrs, the pink and white acacias, purple jacarandas, heralded the hot weather, too hot for pampered racehorses and Dark Invader was taken by Sadiq and Ali and led over the bridge of boats that spanned the Hooghly and through crowded streets to Howrah Station. There he was loaded into a massive horse-box with padded partitions and the railway trundled him majestically to the cooler low-lying hill town of Bangalore and the Quillan stables there. His ex-shipmates stayed behind, being already far enough forward in training to be entered among thinning fields for the last races of the Winter Season, but a few chosen ones went as well, including Flashlight, and a fidgety chestnut called Firefly that Lady Mehta had impetuously bought for fifteen thousand rupees after, by a fluke, it had won the King Edward Cup. "He won't again," predicted John.

With the horses went, with reluctance, Gog and Magog, a yearly ritual. "Big dogs can't stay down in the hot weather," John explained to Ted. "They wouldn't survive." He did not say how much he missed them – his 'mates' he could almost have called them. It was part of the penalty of living in Calcutta.

Ted was in charge and would be in Bangalore to continue the patient day-in, day-out training and supervision and Ted took, too, the three eldest of the bandar-log to go to boarding school. "Poor school," said Bunny. John himself hardly knew his two sons in grey flannel shorts, grey shirts and jerseys, school ties – "Ties!" said John – or his daughter in a blue pleated skirt, blue blouse with a sailor collar and a straw hat – "A *hat*!"

Dahlia wept but, "If you settles down and behaves proper," promised Ted, "I'll take you out every Saturday and give you a sausage tea." Sausages had only entered their lives with Ted; though they could be bought tinned, they were out of Dahlia's ken; to the bandar-log they were delectable.

Now, in late June, John had travelled down to see them, but, he had to own, more importantly to see

Dark Invader and to bring Ted the application forms for him to sign. "You just sign here – and here – and here," John said.

When John had told Ted, the little man had got up from his chair, stared incredulously, swallowed, then walked to the office window and stood with his back to John for at least three minutes. Then, "You mean I can really ride again?" As he turned, the blue eyes were wet.

"Not only ride. You will be up on Dark Invader."

"Dark Invader!" Ted sounded as if he were in a dream.

"Yes." John was deliberately brisk. "You are being retained by Mr. Leventine as his jockey – with an increase of pay, of course. You will bring the horses back in September and we start Darkie in October. The Alipore Stakes, I think, Class IV. Of course, he'll run away with it, then we shall see what we shall see."

"We'll see." Ted's voice was firm now. Then, "May I ask you, sir – was it you who thought of this about my ticket?"

"Not me. Mr. Leventine."

"Mr. Leventine! Did this for me!"

"Wake up, Ted. Mr. Leventine didn't do it for you. He did it for himself. He doesn't *give* favours away."

That was true. Just before they had left for Bangalore, Mr. Leventine, down on the racecourse, had called Ted aside. "You have been so excellent with the horse I should like to give you this," but Ted had backed away from the wad of notes.

"Very kind of you, sir, but I don't need nothing. It's what *you* done for the Invader, sir, that counts."

"Not without you. I know. I have watched," and Mr. Leventine said at his most beguiling, "Please, Mullins," but Ted still shook his head.

"What am I to do with this then?"

"Tell you what." Ted was still haunted by what he had seen on that journey from the docks, what he saw every day as he and Dark Invader crossed the road, and, "If you wants to make me happy," he told Mr. Leventine, "give it to the R.S.P.C.A. for the ponies and buffaloes and oxes and – oh yes! – to them nuns where Mrs. Quillan goes and they feeds the old. *That* would be something." Ted was carried away. "You're so rich, sir. Think what you could give."

"Give!" Mr. Leventine's voice rose with horror. "If I am rich it's because my money is for *use*, to reward those who are worthy, not for *derelicts*," said Mr. Leventine.

"Not even for them what suffers through no fault of their own?" Ted's voice had changed too and was oddly stern. "Me and Ella, my wife, we had a donkey once, beaten almost to death it had been. We had four cats – strays covered with sores they was." Ted stopped. Then, "You rescued Dark Invader."

"Rescued? By no means. I bought him for my own advantage. I believe in that horse."

"And God bless you for that," said Ted. "But . . ." He looked at the notes again. "Give it to R.S.P.C.A., sir."

Mr. Leventine put the wad back in his pocket.

*

"Suffer through no fault of their own." It had been a terrible hot summer in Calcutta; the rains were late in breaking, "which puts the Monsoon Meeting all out of gear," said John. "Which means there might be famine," said Mother Morag in dread – she had lived through two famines. Already the price of rice was high and peasants had begun flocking in from the villages, always an alarming sign. "They hope for work or food and there isn't any." They swelled the lines waiting at the Sisters' street kitchens. "I had hoped we could have opened another in Bow Bazaar," she had told the Community. "I'm afraid we can't," and, "Thank God for our 'collecting'," she said. "At least we can feed our people in the Home," but the collections had lessened. Few people went to restaurants in the heat and, "Solomon is so slow," said Sister Timothea. It was all the Sister said, but Mother Morag knew how punishing was 'collecting' in the heat, especially wearing the habit which, though in India made of white cotton, had not changed since the days of Thérèse Hubert: long-sleeve, high-necked, coming down to the ankles and finished by the close fitting muslin coif, as worn by a Belgian peasant woman in the 1840s. "But that was in *Europe*," Sister Joanna had not quite learned the utter disregard of self. "This is India! Those starched white strings under our chins!"

"They don't stay starched for long," Mother Morag consoled her and laughed. "You should see yours now – spotted with gravy!"

"From the curry canister. Ugh!" It had been Sister Joanna's turn that early dawn to help carry the

105

canisters in. "Curry of all things! I must smell." As they talked they were still storing the food and she saw, when Mother Morag lifted her arms to set some sweet puddings on a high shelf out of the way of ants, how, when her sleeves fell back, the white skin of her arms was covered in scarlet from prickly heat and Sister Joanna was ashamed of her own small grumbling but, tactfully, all she said was, "I had better put on a fresh bonnet to go round the offices this afternoon, or I shall hardly impress the young men," and tried to laugh too.

It was, though, no joke. In these stifling nights sometimes the food had gone bad before Solomon and the cart reached home. No wonder – one night it was after two o'clock. "Well, it's too hot to sleep anyhow," said Sister Ursule. "We might as well be up," but, "How long have we had Solomon?" Mother Morag asked Sister Ignatius next day.

"It must be ten or eleven years."

"And he wasn't all that young when he came."

"No, he was a gift." Like the wise older Sister, Mother Morag knew that people do not give young horses away, and she looked thoughtfully at the dip in Solomon's back, his legs that had thickened; though he still kept his high step, it was awkward and growing stiff. The hollows over his eyes were deep now and, in spite of Gulab's grooming, his coat was rough. Mother Morag sighed and a pucker, what the Sisters called her 'worry line', showed between her eyebrows.

*

The rains broke, to the relief of everyone and everything. "You can almost hear the plants drinking," said Sister Barbara and, "I want to dance in the puddles," said young Sister Mary Fanny, as the bandar-log did up the road. There were brief furious deluges of almost vertical rain, then blue skies with piled up clouds that would presently burst again, but meanwhile the whole earth steamed as the water dried. Colours of grass, trees and flowers shone vivid and glistened in the washed light. The Convent, Scattergold Hall, all the old houses smelled dank; green stains appeared on the walls and mildew on shoes and books, anything leather, "including saddles and harness," said John.

Racing began on the Monsoon Track, sometimes run in a downpour when the jockeys wore celluloid motor-goggles and came in soaking, mud bespattered, their silks clinging to their backs. Few of the outside owners were there, not Lady Mehta, nor John's Nawab, nor Mr. Leventine. The Monsoon Meeting was casual, friendly; it was too hot for raincoats, so members sheltered under golf umbrellas to distinguish them from the crowd's bazaar black ones. Everyone knew everyone else – except for John. For him, as for other trainers, the Monsoon was an anxious time; the early British had called it 'the sickly season', and it was sickly still. "I seem to do nothing but scratch one horse after another from a race," said John. Captain Mack was called out night and day.

"Racehorses! What about humans?" said Sister Ignatius. There were 'ten-day fevers': chills: pleurisy. The old people, even in the Home and under the

Sisters' care, died as easily as flies. "As soon as a bed is empty there are twenty waiting to fill it," and it was not only the old people; the babies died too, and children . . . Mother Morag was too harried to have time to think about Solomon.

Then it seemed to her only a matter of weeks, though it was almost three months when, looking down from her window to watch John Quillan's horses pass, she saw he had a greatly augmented line; augmented too, by horses of a different quality and, after them, kept well back as usual, because his stride outdistanced every other, the big dark horse she had noticed before and the little English rider she knew was Ted Mullins.

"Nervous?" asked John, but Ted gave one of his rare smiles. "Not with him."

Ted had ridden in the first two of the Cold Weather Meetings, but not on Dark Invader. His first ride on the opening Saturday was Mr. Leventine's Pandora – the mare who had come out on the same ship, while Ching rode her companion Pernambuco. Pandora had won. On the second Saturday, at Ted's suggestion, he and Ching changed mounts, Pandora had won again, while Ted rode Pernambuco into second place. The same afternoon, to Lady Mehta's joy, he had brought Flashlight up to win the mile long Jaisalmir Plate. "Up Quillans!" Bunny was bubbling over with congratulations for his friend but, "Wait," said John. "The crux hasn't come yet." The crux was the first appearance of Dark Invader.

As John had said, it was a Class IV race, "but there's a huge field," he told Ted. "They have had to make two divisions." Dark Invader was in Division I with top weight, "but compared to the others you're on a flying machine," John told Ted. "All the same," he added, "it's often the cold-stone certainty that comes unstuck."

"He won't," said Ted. Ted had weighed out, carried his saddle and number-cloths through the door and handed them to John. He, himself, was smart and dapper, his breeches made as a special order by Barkat Ali in Park Street. "I would have had them made in London if we could have been sure of the fit," Mr. Leventine had said. Ted's boots, though, had been sent out from Maxwell's, copied from a pair he had worn in the old days. Mr. Leventine's colours were pink, with emerald hoops, and green cap, and were so bright they made Ted blink. "Pink for happiness, green for hope," Mr. Leventine had explained but, "Hullo, Rosebud! Ain't she sweet!" jeered the other jockeys, but as the horses came into the paddock, there was no mistaking that Dark Invader, with his size, his blooming coat, was outstandingly the best-looking horse on the course; led by Sadiq, murmurs of admiration followed him as he walked round, and soon he had moved up to odds on favourite.

As Ted was swung into the saddle he met Mr. Leventine's gaze, full of a confidence and belief that had not been given Ted since Ella died – he had to turn his own eyes away – but John Quillan still had his doubts and, walking beside Dark Invader as the horses moved out, again he gave Ted his anxious final orders: "Keep clear. If they crowd you, go for the outside rail. Remember you have twenty lengths in hand. Use them. Keep clear."

Only once did Ted steal a look under his elbow at the tailing field behind him. Already two lengths clear, he took the inner rail and kept that distance, finishing, hard held, in a time that – sure as eggs is eggs, thought Ted – would take Dark Invader to Class III. "Exactly as we wished him to do," Mr. Leventine beamed and even John was pleased.

It was a pattern set for the six races that followed, six that for Dark Invader were little more than training gallops; each time he got away to a good start and was never headed, which brought him from Class III to Class II. "As we expected," said Mr. Leventine, rubbing his hands.

Mr. Leventine did not live in one of Calcutta's mansions which, to people who did not really know him, would have seemed suited to his wealth and ostentatious tastes. Mr. Leventine detested waste and, "What would one man do with twenty rooms?" he would have asked. One day he might marry but now he had no time; he had little time too for gardens, trees, lawns, and none at all for the hangers-on that always come with vast houses. He was perfectly content with a flat in a modern block on Park Street, but took the precaution of renting the flat above his so that he would not be annoyed by noise or other tenants. His two secretaries were allowed to live there, but had to walk about in socks or slippers and speak in whispers. He also rented the flat below, where he put his chauffeur, his car attendant and his personal bearers – it needed two to keep his clothes as he thought fit and, "I don't want them smelling of servants' quarters, of cooking and biris."

Now in his library, he moved all his racing cups to a side table and kept his mantelpiece only for Dark Invader's; already there were three, only of Indian silver it was true, but there was also a gilt quaich. He had to ask John to explain what the Scots drinking cup was. "A tassie," John had said, to tease him – Mr. Leventine could not find 'tassie' in the dictionary. There was a two-handled goblet, sterling silver this time and, most handsome of all, a rosebowl. "You *are* coming up," said Bunny. Mr. Leventine felt he could ask Bunny and, now and then, John to come and drink his excellent whisky. There was nobody else. One day, if Dark Invader succeeded, perhaps Sir Humphrey . . . but that was a dream. Meanwhile here was Bunny and, "You must keep a place for the gold one," said Bunny with his usual sunniness. Mr. Leventine, superstitious to his backbone, almost said, "Hush," but, "He's just doing what we expected," was all he said.

What no-one had expected was the impact of Dark Invader on the crowd. Though, after his first win, the odds offered on him would have made nobody's fortune, the whole of racing Calcutta seemed to have taken him to their hearts. It was partly his size and his good looks, partly the way in which, once he had won, instead of coming in with his ears still intent, he let them flop as if to say, "That's that," tucked in his chin modestly as if to say, "It's nothing at all," and would not wait to nuzzle Mr. Leventine's pockets. He and Ted had swiftly become a legend and stories were told of how Darkie would race for no-one else, nor even let anyone ride or so much as mount him: of his extraordinary intelligence: his laziness – "He doesn't bother to try at gallops. Why should he? He knows he can when it's the real thing": of his greediness and how the salty taste of Bengal straw had once induced him to eat his bedding and how he would have died of colic if Captain Mack had not dramatically saved him – this happened to be true and, after that, Dark Invader was bedded on tan-bark: of his exceptional docility and good nature – as long as he was not ridden by anyone else but Ted.

Ted had difficulty, not only on race days, but in the early mornings, of getting the Invader through the admirers who wanted to see and pat him. "Just like a matinée idol outside a stage door," said John. On race days he had to ask for a police escort and for every race Dark Invader was entered, there came, from the Public Enclosure and the frenzied dust-coloured crowds that lined the rails, a chant for Darkie. A mounted policeman, conspicuous in his white starched tunic and scarlet turban, would often have to turn his horse backwards to the people to let it kick out and drive them back from surging on to the course itself. As soon as Dark Invader appeared, the people would begin with single shouts as his great striding form showed clear of the field along the back stretch. "Darkee!" "Darkee!" they would call and then, as he came storming past the stands, they would break into a quick-fire rhythm, "Dark Invader, Dark Invader, Dark Invader."

Mr. Leventine would be out on the course to lead him in, Ted, in his over-brilliant silks, perched firmly on top, lifting his whip in shy salute. Dark Invader would tuck in his chin and lop his ears in acknowledgement of the applause before his search for tidbits and the crowd would grow wild.

"Your horse seems to have become something of a personality," Sir Humphrey sought Mr. Leventine out at the Club. "You know he's now eligible for the Viceroy's Cup?"

"I know." Mr. Leventine had a new dignity, while even John Quillan betrayed a fresh buoyancy. "I believe, Sandy," he said to Captain Mack at Scattergold Hall, "that the time is coming when you may have to eat your hat."

"Willingly," said Captain Mack. "What fun if Ted beats all the top-price English jockeys who'll be brought out for the big races."

V

On the eve of December 21st which, as the Sisters knew, was St. Thomas's Day, a full moon looked down over Calcutta.

It was well after midnight and the morning mist was beginning to form on the river, spreading softly over the banks and the wide flatness of the Maidan, filling the star-shaped moat of the Fort, swirling up the lower tiers of the stands on the racecourse, laying a white carpet round the domed marble of the Victoria Memorial and the spired gothic of the Cathedral.

In the bedroom of his flat in Park Street, Mr. Leventine lay alone in his large carved mahogany bed over which his mosquito net hung from a vast frame; in fact, everything in the flat was vast. The room was lined with massive Victorian wardrobes with full length mirrors, others were in his dressing-room where his dressing-table was divided by another looking glass; his silver brushes, and bottles with silver tops shone. The wardrobes were full of well-pressed suits, their exteriors were polished and the floors of imitation stone were burnished to a red gloss.

His bathroom held a huge porcelain bath set in mahogany and in his elaborate basin the humble plug was replaced by a column operated by knobs and levers, all silver plated. The lavatory might have been designed for the hams of a race of giants; the pan had a pattern of pink tulips and green leaves. In all this splendour Mr. Leventine could not sleep. Why not? He had an invaluable capacity, taught him by his mother, of 'switching off' and falling at once to sleep. As in his childhood, he still reached up to an imaginary electric light switch, to flick it off. He had done the same tonight, but it had not worked.

The evening before, after Bunny had gone, Mr. Leventine, glass in hand, had stood looking at the mantelpiece. Bunny's friendliness had filled him with such cheer that suddenly he had been moved to rearrange the cups – goblets to the left, the quaich and rosebowl on the right, in the middle an empty space and, "It will be gold," Mr. Leventine had whispered.

"It will be gold." Seldom had he felt as confident, as full of cheer; that night he had slept like a child, but tonight he was uneasy. Why? asked Mr. Leventine.

The moon shone down on the Quillan stables; on the lawns and across the track it threw long shadows of trees, shadows too on the verandahs that ran around the stalls but the light picked out the blanketed forms of the syces where they lay, each with a lantern turned low beside his charpoy. The coming champion or hope of India was not asleep; Dark Invader was on his knees on the tan-bark of his bedding, straining with a total loss of dignity to reach an odd straw which had escaped his neighbour's stall, elongating his lips till he looked like his distant South American relative, the tapir. Finally, resigned to failure, he sighed deeply, rose to his feet, drooped his lower lip and slept.

The bedrooms of Scattergold Hall were empty. December 20th was Dahlia's father's birthday and, by Quillan tradition, John drove her, the children, the latest baby and Gog and Magog to Burdwan where Mr. McGinty worked, as many Eurasians did, on the railway.

John's car was an old four-seater Chrysler. "1922 model," John purposely told Mr. Leventine. Its wooden spoked wheels needed water poured on them in hot weather; its broad back seat held children, dogs, bags of oats or bales of hay, kittens, luggage, parcels, and it ran accompanied by a steady thump from the engine like an elderly tramp steamer. The children loved it and all the year, Dahlia, as John knew, looked forward to this day. Burdwan was one of the biggest junctions, and its Institute or Eurasian Club was crowded so that there she saw many of her once-upon-a-time people as well as her father and mother – uncles and aunts, great-uncles, great-aunts, troops and troops of cousins and friends – because in the evening they always went to the Institute, the railway workers' club, and Dahlia could show off her John and their children, who equally shrank from it but, as if drawn by an unspoken love, went through it with a grace that no-one would have believed of them. John joked, laughed, danced, even sang, while the bandars submitted to Dahlia's idea of lacy frilled dresses and sashes, white shorts and shirts and bow ties, "like little gentlemen". There was always a dinner, elaborate as only Dahlia's mother could make it and the Quillans always stayed the night.

With Eurasian voices still shrilling in his ears John slept fitfully in his parents-in-law's big bed – touchingly, they always insisted on moving out of it for John and Dahlia. She lay softly against him, blissfully asleep, and softly against her lay their newest baby. Prolific as her name-flower, Dahlia had just produced their eighth child; "another little calamity", Babu Ram Sen had said, which meant another daughter and, in Ram Sen's thinking, another dowry to be found, but John was not thinking of dowries – "There won't be any, anyway" – he was worried about the present. He should not really have left the stables this year, so much was at stake, but it was Dahlia's day, one out of three hundred and sixty-five, and John comforted himself with the thought that Ted was there. John had given careful orders, "and I shall be back soon after nine," he had told Ted. "The baby wakes us at dawn." 'Never, never should the baby be allowed to sleep in its mother's bed,' said the books, but Dahlia never read books and all her babies slept with her, "which is why they don't give any trouble," said Dahlia.

"The trouble comes later on," said John wryly but now, careful not to disturb her, he reached across Dahlia and, with a deftness that no-one would have believed of that once fastidious and cynical young cavalry officer, covered and tucked in the sleeping baby with its shawl. The baby blew a contented bubble from its lips and, "Ted's there. It must be all right," and John too went to sleep.

*

117

Ted was not asleep. He was sitting on his small verandah and, though his jersey was thin and he had no coat, he did not feel the cold, nor the mosquitoes biting. He was past feeling anything.

It had been a bad day which was odd because the bad day should have been yesterday, the anniversary of his and Ella's wedding. Ted seldom spoke on that day and always tried to keep it properly as he had done when Ella was alive. Here in Calcutta, in the midst of all the excitement, he had taken out their wedding photograph from the small tin trunk that held all his possessions and put the silver-framed picture beside his bed, a vase of sweet peas in front of it. The bandar-log had been much interested. "But why is she wearing a lace curtain on her head?" asked one of the boys. It was an innocent question – none of them had seen an English wedding – but then the eldest girl had looked more closely and, "You told us Mrs Ella was pretty," she said accusingly. "She was, to me." "Well, I think she's ugly." Ted had snatched the photograph away and given the little girl a slap. It was the first time he had slapped a child and it was too hard. She burst into tears, tears hurt and surprised and with one accord the bandars deserted Ted. They had not been near him since and had gone to Burdwan without saying goodbye.

To be truthful, yesterday, apart from the ritual of the photograph and flowers, Ted had not thought much about Ella until the evening. Yesterday he had eaten his solitary dinner quite cheerfully – tonight he had sent it away. Usually after dinner he played snakes and ladders, or draughts, or cards with the

118

children, at which they were adept, but yesterday there had been no children; he had not wanted to go to bed and, after a time, a strange restlessness, uncommon after a day's work, had driven him to walk in the garden. He had meant to think about Ella but, about eleven o'clock the old Chrysler turned in at the gates and he saw it was Mr. Quillan – not only he, but Mrs. Quillan, which was uncommon. He could not remember Mrs. Quillan going out at night, but Bunny had given a pre-Christmas dinner and insisted that Dahlia should come. "Don't be stuffy, John. I like Dahlia and I want her." Dahlia had been enchanted. "Out two nights running! My God!" and John had let her buy a new dress and evening cloak at Mrs. Woods's shop on Park Street.

John always drove himself and when he had put the car away, he and Dahlia had walked back through the garden to the house. They had passed close by Ted who had stepped back behind a screen of bougainvillaea; beside him was another plant that drenched the air with such sweetness he felt giddy. Dahlia paused; it was seldom that she was out so late. "What is that perfume?" "Queen of the Night," said John, "rat ki rani," and Dahlia had echoed, "Queen of the Night".

Ted could see her clearly; her bare arms and neck – the light where the moon caught her hair – Dahlia was always especially radiant after the birth of a child. The new dress, a confection of taffeta and lace in her favourite apricot, had a silken rustle as she moved; the cloak had slipped down as she turned to John. The two of them clung close, then John put his hand under her chin and bent his head to kiss her. Ted had heard the kiss. He could not bear to watch. His eyes had been burning and he had hastily gone inside.

Next afternoon the Quillan family left for Burdwan.

"I hate to go," John told Ted, "but I know you will take charge. Captain Mack will come and support you for the evening parade, His Highness too," – if Bunny remembers, thought John – "and you will have Ching and the Jemadar. Here are the morning orders." He went through the list with Ted: which riding boy was to ride what horse: Ching's rides: how they should ride: matched with whom, and for how long: even what Ted was to do with Dark Invader, "and I should be glad if you will take Firefly yourself. That horse is a problem. We shall leave Burdwan about six, so I should be back by nine."

"Yes, sir."

"If anything is the least wrong, tell the babu to ring Captain Mack."

"Yes, sir, but I'm sure there won't be."

"And Ted, last thing, will you do the stable night round?"

The night round had been the last straw. It meant Ted had to sit up late and the hours seemed endless. Scattergold Hall, usually overflowing with life, was silent, empty. The servants had taken the opportunity of an evening off and gone to their quarters. The gates were shut. Ted had taken John's electric torch – even though there was moonlight he needed to look deep into each stall – and faithfully he went from one to the next, all around the square, stepping softly, careful not to disturb the sleeping grooms and horses. When

he came to Dark Invader, the Invader was too lazy
even to raise his head or give his customary whinny
and, with Sadiq's charpoy across the stall's front, Ted
could not reach to pat and fondle him. "Real old
canoodler he is," Ted had often said. Now, "'Used to
be' is nearer the mark," Ted said bitterly and, what he
had not felt for a long time, jealousy came back and,
added to it, hurt. Ted passed on to the next horse but
the smart of the hurt went on and, when he went back
to his solitary room, he sat at his table, his head in his
hands.

Somewhere a drum was being beaten and voices
were chanting in a nasal whine, utterly alien. There
was a smell of dust and of pungent cooking, of hookah
smoke and a waft of unbearable sweetness from that
flower, Queen of the Night. He could hear Dahlia's
soft voice saying its name after John – Dahlia's voice,
not Ella's – and such desolation and longing fell on
Ted that he shuddered. It was then that he
remembered Mr. Leventine's whisky.

Mr. Leventine had come when the parade was over
and the owners and their friends had gone. "I 'spect to
them cocktail dos," Ted had told him.

Mr. Leventine had been put out not to find John
there. "I don't have to tell him my every movement,"
John would have said. "He may have bought Dark
Invader, but he hasn't bought me." John would have
been disarmed though, because a Father Christmas
Mr. Leventine had brought wonderful presents. The
Minerva was loaded.

Sadiq was presented with a gold watch, Ali with one
in silver. "A nice distinction," John said afterwards.

121

There were toys for the children, large dolls and teddy bears, clockwork trains, boxes of soldiers and air-guns. "For Gawd's sake, don't give them those, sir," begged Ted.

"Not?" Mr. Leventine was sad. He liked air-guns. "Not?"

"No, sir." Ted was firm.

Large boxes of chocolates were handed out for everyone. For Dahlia there was a bouquet of orchids and a case of champagne: for John a case of whisky, "the very best Scotch," Ted said reverently. "What a pity the family's out, sir. Never mind. It will be all the more surprise." He helped Mr. Leventine, the chauffeur and the car attendant to arrange the gifts in the sitting-room, the toys and chocolate boxes piled around the cases, Dahlia's orchids on top, set off by an enormous card printed in gold with a photograph of Dark Invader. Ted had one too and, with it, an English racing saddle. Nothing could have pleased Ted more; every jockey of prestige had his own saddle, but Ted's was one John had bought for him in Dhurrumtollah Street. This was by a leading English maker. "As if you hadn't done enough for me, sir! Too generous you are by half!" and Mr. Leventine was filled with an extraordinary glow. No-one had called him generous before – "How could they?" Bunny would have said – and, "It gives me great pleasure," Mr. Leventine told Ted and, to his astonishment, found that it was true.

*

The glow had faded; in fact, as he lay sleepless, Mr. Leventine was remembering all the money he had needlessly spent and chided himself for it. His usual astuteness seemed to have deserted him. He was more accustomed to say, "Done with you," "It's a bargain," or "Raise you five," than "It gives me great pleasure," and, "Casimir Alaric Bruce," Mr. Leventine addressed himself – his mother used to call him by all his names when she was severely displeased – "You are becoming soft and silly. Be yourself."

Still he tossed and turned and then a chill small wind seemed to come into his bedroom. "A warning?" asked Mr. Leventine.

Suddenly he sat up, pressed down the imaginary switch, got out of bed, lifted the net and, in his black satin pyjamas, with a twined monogram, C.A.B.L., embroidered in orange on the pocket, padded into the library and hastily put Dark Invader's trophies back in their original order on the mantelpiece.

A case of whisky.

Ted remembered what Michael Traherne had said when he had seen Ted and Dark Invader on board the *City of London* and gone down to Ted's cabin to say goodbye. "Life on board ship can be very boring, and very tempting," Michael had said. "But, Ted, if there's the least sign of trouble," and Ted knew Michael meant 'his trouble', "you will be put ashore at Malta, Naples, Port Said, Colombo or wherever, and left to make your own way home. More than that, another lad – and we can't guarantee what sort of lad – will have to take over Darkie."

Ted had not protested, sworn off, done any of the things most of the men would have done but had stood straighter and looked at Michael with his blue eyes hard. "I haven't touched a drop, sir, since the day you put me on the Invader. Nor will I," but he was not on board ship now, and he had lost Dark Invader. Ted forgot their new partnership, even more intimate than the companionship of horse and lad; a companionship of work. He forgot how the crowds now could not think of them apart. He only knew that his Invader had not whinnied to him, that Sadiq was between them. "Should have been glad he was so healthily asleep," he told himself, "and that Mr. Saddick looks after him so well." It did not stop the jealousy, nor the ache of loneliness and suddenly Ted was angry. Mr. Quillan shouldn't have put all this on him. It was too much responsibility. He was too old for the crowds shouting "Darkie, Darkie," while Mr. Quillan poured instructions into his ear. Mr. Leventine was suddenly too overwhelming, expected too much. Sadiq was a usurper and everyone had gone off leaving him, Ted, in this empty house and that child had been rude about Ella – Ella who now seemed further away than ever – and all the time the drum went on and on. "That damned drum!" Ted shouted it aloud but there was no-one to hear him; in fact, his own voice came back to him in an echo from the garden's high wall – "Drum . . . drum".

Ted got up, went into the sitting-room, opened John's case, carefully lifting the orchids aside and took out a bottle of whisky. "Just for a nip . . . just one. Mr. Quillan wouldn't grudge me that."

Some time later, he had no idea how much later, a thought struck Ted. "Haven't done the stable night round. Mus' do that. Promised." He stumbled up and again took the torch but, from sitting on the cold verandah his hands were numb and he could hardly hold it. His teeth chattered and he shook with cold. "Better have another drink to warm me," but the bottle was empty. Ted cursed and almost tumbled down the steps. The moonlight was brilliant on the lawn and track, but the shadows were dark as fallen trees on pools, which Ted thought they really were and, trying to avoid them, he seemed to be going zigzag; nor could he keep the quiet stealth. Twice he dropped the torch, swore loudly, and heads began to lift on the charpoys. When he came to Dark Invader his anger overcame him and he shook Sadiq. "Out of my way, you heathen. Lemme see my hoss."

At first Sadiq could not take it in. In his shirt, barefooted, his brown-yellow eyes blurred with sleep, he looked a different man without his turban and, "Who are you?" bellowed Ted. "How did you get in here?" and, "Thief!" he shouted. "Thief!" Clumsily he shook the top rail of the stall, trying to get it down and Sadiq sprang to life. His muscular arm seized Ted. "Sahib! Ted *Sahib* . . . Sahib! No!"

For a moment Ted sobered. Then, "Mind your own bloody business."

Holding him, Sadiq tried to summon his English. "Sahib, this no good. No . . . no, Sahib. I no like. Quillan Sahib no like. No good him." He motioned at Dark Invader who had woken up and was watching puzzled. "Night round been done . . . bed now,

Sahib. You ride tomorrow – please, Ted Sahib."

"Oh, go to hell!" Ted shook off Sadiq and turned back, but not to his verandah – to the house where he took out another bottle. He could not open it and, back on his verandah, smashed the neck against a verandah post; nor could he pour the whisky out into his glass but managed to put the bottle on the table where it stood running whisky while Ted fell into his chair. The drum was beating in his head now; the flower scent was overpowering. Ted was sick, then collapsed across the table.

It was Sadiq, touching Ted as if with a pair of tongs, the end of his turban wound over his mouth and nose to keep out the stench of vomit and, to a Muslim, the abominable smell of alcohol, who put Ted to bed.

Three o'clock. Half past three. Four o'clock. The Sisters Ursule and Jane, Gulab, Solomon and the cart had not come in. Since midnight Mother Morag had been up; twice she had sent Dil Bahadur down the road to see – he had been as far as Chowringhee – no sign, and for the last hour she had been walking up and down, up and down. Sister Barbara and Sister Emmanuel whose turn it was to help unload, puzzled at not being called, had risen themselves and were with her; presently Sister Ignatius, who seemed to know by instinct when anything was wrong, had appeared. "What can have happened?"

"Something." Mother Morag dared say no more.

"An accident?"

"The police would have come."

"Solomon?" asked Sister Ignatius.

"It can't be Solomon," said Sister Barbara, "he's so reliable."

'No-one can be reliable for ever."

At last they heard the sound of wheels – the gates had long been open – and, with the wheels, a hubbub: murmurs, talking, shouted orders, the babel of a crowd. When, with the Sisters, she hurried to the courtyard, Mother Morag had need of all her calm. Both Sisters, Jane and Ursule, were walking, their faces pallid with sweat, their coifs fallen back, cloaks and habits bedraggled. With them was a band of coolies, those men who, in India, always seem to spring from the ground when there is something to be done, a few annas to be earned, as did small boys – there were a dozen or more small boys – all of them were helping to hold up the shafts of the cart, and the shafts were holding up Solomon, whom Gulab held by the bridle, trying to support his head. Carefully the men eased the cart into the courtyard, unbuckled the harness and lowered the shafts.

"Mother, he fell just past Dhurrumtollah," Sister Jane tried to keep her voice even, but it came in distressed gasps. "We thought he had just slipped – the police helped to get him up and Gulab walked beside him. Then again, outside Firpo's, when we came out with the canisters – it seemed he couldn't move. We thought we shouldn't try to collect any more." Sister Jane's voice was stilled by a sob and Sister Ursule went on. "We were nearly at the end in any case – but, Mon Dieu! to get him home!"

"It was so cruel, but we thought it best to get help."

Sister Jane was really crying now. "Oh Mother!"

Solomon was standing curiously rigid, his tail at an extraordinary high angle: his lips were drawn back showing the yellowed teeth and flecks of froth came between them. "Aie! Aie!" the pitying voices sounded as the men pressed round. Dil Bahadur had to take his cane to hold them back. When she made her way through, Mother Morag saw with horror that the old horse was twitching with curious spasms, sweat broke out on his shoulders and neck and as she went swiftly to him she saw he could not bend it as Gulab tried to unbuckle the bridle. To the Sisters' astonishment she went round in front of the old horse and gave him a sharp tap on the forehead. "Mother! To punish him *now*!" but Mother Morag had seen what she had guessed she must see, an immediate flash across the eyeball. She tapped again, it came again and, "Unmistakable," said Mother Morag. "Sister Barbara, ring Captain Mack and tell him to come at once "

"Yes. Tetanus," said Captain Mack. "Poor old boy. I had thought it would be old age."

The sight of tetanus is not pretty and sharply Mother Morag sent the, by now, thoroughly roused Community inside.

"Sister Jane, Sister Ursule must both have a wash and some good strong tea. Sister Emmanuel will you see to that? Plenty of sugar. For Gulab too."

"And I think you should go in yourself, Reverend Mother," said Captain Mack.

"I'll stay." Mother Morag had one hand on Solomon's neck.

"Stand away from him."

There was a short sharp noise in the courtyard, a ring of iron on stone and the sound of something soft and heavy falling. Gulab burst into loud, uncontrollable sobs. Dil Bahadur led him away through the now silent coolies and boys. "Sister will bring him some tea," Mother Morag told Dil Bahadur.

It was she who helped Captain Mack cover the still heap with a tarpaulin the Captain fetched from his car. "I'll arrange the rest," he told her.

"Thank you." She knew, with him, she had no need to say more than that and, as his car drove away, she called the Sisters. "I think it would be good if we all helped to unload the cart."

"*Unload! After this?*" The Sisters were shocked.

"Of course. We're not going to let Solomon's last effort go to waste, but Sister Ursule and Sister Jane must go to bed."

"Please no, Mother. We couldn't sleep just yet."

The coolies who had lingered for the drama came to help with the unloading and, with so many people, the work was quickly done and it was then that Sister Mary Fanny said timidly, "Would it be very silly, Mother, if we went into the chapel and said a prayer?"

"For Solomon?" Mother Morag smiled down at her Sister. "I don't think it would be at all silly. Come – and, child, fetch Gulab and Dil Bahadur."

"A Hindu in our chapel! And I don't know what denomination Dil Bahadur is . . ." Sister Ignatius was of the old narrow school. "Thank God for bigotry," she often said. "It keeps our faith pure," but, "I think it would help Gulab," said Mother Morag and, indeed, Sister Mary Fanny found the old man sobbing, face downward in the straw of Solomon's bedding. Dil Bahadur could not come because the crowd had not dispersed but, "They say they pray too," said Dil Bahadur.

"Hindu prayers!" sniffed Sister Ignatius.

"Prayers," Mother Morag corrected her. "Sister, those men who are so poor would not take an anna for what they did for us and Solomon tonight – and don't you think we shall need all the prayers we can get?"

It was while they were in the chapel that they heard the iron wheels of a heavy cart backing into the courtyard, then the grinding of a winch and the sound of wheels departing. There was a fresh burst of weeping from some of the Sisters, from Gulab too. Mother Morag gave the 'knock'. "Bed everyone," she said, "and this morning, meditation will be after Mass, so you will have half an hour's extra sleep."

As there was now no more to be seen in the courtyard, the crowd dispersed. Dil Bahadur took Gulab into his gatehouse and shut the door. The Sisters had left the chapel but Mother Morag stayed on.

In all her sadness, shock and pain, as Superior she had to ask herself the question, "How, *how* are we going to replace Solomon?" The Convent's small money savings had disappeared in the high price of rice. There was nothing to spare. "I shall have to apply to the General Fund,' murmured Mother Morag, something the Sisters of Poverty tried their utmost not to do. "It has so many calls on it." Each house tried to live by donations and by its own 'collecting', but how could they collect without a Solomon? They could hire a tikka gharry, but that would be expensive and the poor half-starved waifs of animals who drew them could never stand up to the night round. "We need a strong well-trained horse with good blood in him, but the cost of that would be perhaps several hundred rupees." Mother Morag shut her eyes.

She felt a rustle beside her. It was Sister Ursule. "Mother, please allow me. I could not sleep." Then Sister Ignatius came; Sister Mary Fanny stole in; Sister Timothea, though it was her night off; Sister Emmanuel, Barbara, Jane, Claudine – the whole Community – and, as if moved by a single thought, they began a novena, the prayer of the Church for a special – and, perhaps, desperate – intention and, "God doesn't think like men and when one belongs to Him, one must not worry." Mother Morag was ashamed of herself.

The Sisters were not the only ones who prayed. When, at dawn, Mother Morag came out into the courtyard, she saw that the dark stain where Solomon had lain was touched with whitewash and there were marigolds strewn over it. It had become a holy place. As she watched, a woman in the poorest of saris came, bringing more flowers and an offering of a small saucer of rice.

"Mother, that surely can't be right – in a Convent?"

"I don't know if it's right, but I do know it is love

and respect," and Mother Morag told Dil Bahadur to keep the gates open.

The bandar-log were the first to visit Ted – they had decided to forgive him. When the old Chrysler arrived at Scattergold Hall, they were tumbled out pell-mell and John drove straight away. The stables were empty of horses so, thinking Ted was with them down on the racecourse, the children went in to breakfast but, like true bandars, they were always the first to pick up an alarm – in this case the underground gossip of the stable and kitchens – and soon they were at the annex. On the verandah table was the early morning tray of tea, toast and bananas, put down by an appalled Ahmed; beside it was the broken-necked bottle of whisky, still three-quarters full, another empty bottle rolled on the ground. They went in to look at Ted, stealing silently up to his bed, half-fascinated, half-repelled. He was lying on his back and snoring; his clothes were on the floor where Sadiq had thrown them. With their small prehensile fingers, the children tried to open Ted's eyes, but he only rolled his head and grunted and a small boy began to cry with fear. Back on the verandah, they wiped their fingers in the whisky spilt on the table, tasted, spat it out and, for once defeated, fled in a troop to tell Dahlia.

"Ted! My God, what have you been doing?" Dahlia took him by the shoulders and shook him, trying to make him sit up, but he sank back as if he were made of rag. "Ted! John will be veree angry. Wake up, Ted. Please to wake." There was no response.

132

She gathered up the clothes. "Take these to the dhobi, the washerman, at once." Ahmed took them at arm's length. Hastily Dahlia searched drawers and put out clean ones. "My God, what will John say?" but John did not come back with the horses, nor did the Jemadar or Sadiq, only Ching and, when Dahlia ran out to him, Ching, unlike his usual courteous self, turned his face away and did not answer. A strange quiet, too, lay over the stables, the men silently going about the morning's rubbing down, the feeds and grooming.

John did not come in for breakfast and Dahlia grew more worried. This could be nothing to do with Ted and even when she heard the car, John did not come into the house. He went straight to the annex. She heard his hard, angry steps.

Ted was awake now, sitting on the edge of his bed, trying to get the walls of his room in focus, but his eyes were fogged. In his head the drum was beating louder than ever, it hurt and his mouth felt foul and dry; he knew that he stank 'in and out'. Then he, too, heard John's steps and gave a small animal whimper.

"So!"

John was in the doorway, his face dark with rage, his voice grim. "So!" The word cut through the air and Ted was suddenly aware how he must look in one of the old-fashioned nightshirts Ella had made him long ago, his lean sinewy legs white and unsightly, his eyes bleared and his hair on end. He was aware, too, of sunlight, so bright outside the door that it made him blink. Then, suddenly, and brutally, more aware, he asked, "Sir, wha's the time?"

"Well after ten o'clock."

"Ten!" Ted shot upright. "Then, sir – I'm too late . . ."

"Too late!" and John laughed, not a pleasant laugh. "You may like to know that in your absence – or because of your absence" – the words cut again – "down on the course Ching changed jockeys with a character you have met already, Streaky Bacon."

"Streaky! *Streaky* – here in Calcutta?" Ted was dazed.

"In Calcutta. English jockeys do come out – unfortunately." John's voice was biting. "The horse threw him and bolted, God knows where. Dark Invader has disappeared. Congratulations."

John went out. If there had been a door he would have slammed it.

"Nobody knows," Mother Morag said often, "who will be asked to do what next!" which tangled sentence was true; but she should have added, "Of course, they must have resource and courage."

At half past seven that morning, a Mr. James Dunn paid his bill at the boarding-house in Lower Circular Road where he always stayed on his unwilling visits to Calcutta, a city he detested. It was the same boarding-house that had welcomed Ted. James Dunn was a plump middle-aged Scotsman of small importance, being the engineer in charge of the jute presses in the jute mills of McKenzie, McNaught and McKenzie at Narayangunj, that town of jute mills, two hundred miles from Calcutta. James Dunn could have gone back there by an overnight train and short steamer journey but, in India, one river leads to another and Narayangunj was on the Luckia, a tributary of the Bhramaputra which flows into the Bay of Bengal, as does the Hooghly, so that James could travel home by river, a slow meandering that he loved. It took eight days and now he was on his way to the river, where a paddle-steamer waited at Chand Pal Ghat on the Strand. To have had a taxi come to the boarding-house would have cost unnecessary money and he set out to catch one at the bottom of the road where it met the racecourse.

Though James Dunn was an undistinguished person, behind him came his bearer, Sohan Lall, carrying his topee – it was too early to wear one – and his coat, and behind Sohan Lall two of the boarding-house coolies carried James's suitcase and canvas hold-all and a small sausage-like bedding roll, Sohan Lall's luggage. James himself carried Calcutta's two daily newspapers, the *Statesman* and the *Englishman*.

For Calcutta, it was a fresh sweet morning; sunlight had begun to filter through the mist that still lay on the racecourse and the Maidan. He liked mist; it reminded him faintly of his native Arbroath and Dundee, though there it was a proper smur, damp and cold. True, the crows were making their usual raucous hawking, a man was hosing unmentionable débris into the gutter, but a dove was calling from a casuarina tree and, over garden walls, James could smell the scent of English flowers. He had breakfasted well, he would soon be safe on the steamer where he could spend Christmas – now only four days off – away from the pseudo-gaiety of an Indian city or town, and James

135

began to whistle 'Ye Banks and Braes o' Bonny Doon'.

There were no taxis at the bottom of the road but, "There'll be plenty in Chowringhee," and the little retinue crossed the road to the turf that edged the racecourse and turned right. It was then that they heard the sound of galloping hooves – hooves not on the racecourse, but on the harder ground on which they stood. The sound came steadily nearer; then, out of the mist, mane and tail flying, they saw a great dark horse.

Even to James Dunn's ignorant eye it was palpably a racehorse, a runaway that had thrown its rider – stirrups and reins were flapping – and it must have jumped the rails. "God Almighty! It's heading towards Chowringhee! The traffic! Trams!" James Dunn cried it aloud.

Already the rhythmic ta-ta-tump on the hard baked earth was loud, getting louder. The horse was bearing down on them where they stood near an intersecting road. The coolies dropped the luggage and fled. "Aie!" cried Sohan Lall and jumped out of reach and, "Ay," said James, the same sound but a different meaning, and he stepped forward, arms extended.

A thoroughbred horse travelling true and determined, ears pricked, at some fifteen miles an hour, is an awkward thing to tackle, even for an expert, and ninety-nine men out of a hundred would, like Sohan Lall, have jumped for safety, but James stood his ground, a folded newspaper in each hand held at arm's length and, "Whoa!" he bellowed. "Whoa!"

There was the sound of hooves slipping on the

tarmac. For a moment James thought the horse would come down, but it dropped its head, planted its feet and slid to a stop. He had a view at close quarters of large furry ears edged with little beads of moisture from the mist, wide nostrils, delicately made, and lustrous eyes. "Stand!" commanded James but, before he could stretch out a hand to catch at the reins, the horse swerved and went past him to the stretch of turf, stopped, looked with its ears pricked forward, then, instead of dashing on to the perils of Chowringhee, turned and walked back. "Yes, *walked*," James Dunn told Sohan Lall; then, as if by intent, crossed the road; for once there were no cars, only a tikka gharry and a rickshaw which it avoided, and began to trot, not fast but purposefully, not far, only a few hundred yards up Lower Circular Road, when it stopped suddenly, turned neatly on its hocks with a grind of steel on stone and cantered in through an open gateway; James, running after it as fast as his plumpness allowed, heard the clatter of its hooves on cobbles.

"Somebody must have guided it," Sister Mary Fanny said. "Must have been an angel," but James Dunn, as he caught up, saw no-one and never knew he, in a way, was the angel. When he reached the gateway there was nothing but the warm sweet smell of horse sweat – "Strange that theirs smells so nice, human's so dreadful," he said to himself. Only the smell and a white scratch on the pavement. There was a gatehouse but no gateman; peering in James could see an old-fashioned cobbled courtyard and an out-building in which was a stall and a conical pile of straw;

a stable certainly but, even to him, not the sort to house a racehorse. He had thought racehorses lived in state in trainers' stables; this was a simple single stall, but the horse had seemed to know exactly where it was going; indeed he could hear the sound of munching – food must have been made ready.

There was a bellpull beside the gateway – James Dunn did not notice the little statue set in the niche below, nor the cross above it; he was debating whether to pull the bell or not. He looked at his watch; there was the steamer to catch and if he pulled the bell he must wait until somebody came and there must be explanations. The horse was safe – he could still hear the munching – and so, still breathing a little hard, a little warm about the collar, he walked back to join Sohan Lall and his luggage by the road.

"Shabash!" said Sohan Lall, which means Bravo! "But Sahib," he added in Hindustani, "You might have been killed."

"Rot!" but, as James Dunn hailed his taxi, he was not whistling 'Ye banks and Braes' but 'Cock o' the North'.

Father Joseph, in his purple vestments, had just turned from the altar to give the Sisters his blessing and said the final words, "Ite missa est" – the Mass is ended – and the Sisters had risen in their ranks to give the answer; those old people who had wanted to come had risen too, others in wheelchairs or even beds that had been wheeled to the tribune or balcony above, bowed their heads. "Deo Gratias" – God be thanked – and, "It was as we said those words," said Sister Mary Fanny, "that we heard it – a loud slither at the gates."

Father Joseph had said a special prayer not, to her disappointment, for the repose of Solomon – "I'm sure he had a soul" – but that the Sisters would be helped in the predicament his death had left. Now, with his small acolyte, a dusky protégé of the nuns, walking in front of him, Father Joseph had started to leave when he stopped, the boy too, while a controlled ripple seemed to run along the rows of nuns as through the chapel windows came the unmistakable sound of horse's hooves on stone. The sound stopped; the priest left and the disciplined Sisters knelt for the Thanksgiving, Mother Morag with them, but she quickly gave the knock, rose and led them out, each Sister trying still to be reverent and not to jostle. They poured into the courtyard and now there was a real ripple – a gasp.

In Solomon's stall was a horse; as it heard them it turned round as if to greet them and they saw its size and splendour. The most beautiful horse they had ever seen.

It was only for a moment – Solomon's feed was not yet quite demolished and then the only sound in the courtyard was a steady munching as the Sisters stood silent in the early sunlight; though some had tears running down their cheeks, their faces were illumined. At last Sister Mary Fanny whispered, "It's a miracle. It *is* a miracle, Mother, isn't it?"

"Not yet." The question had jolted Mother Morag into action, and her voice rang clear and firm. "Wake

Dil Bahadur. Tell him to close the gates and keep them closed," said Mother Morag.

In John Quillan's small office at the stables, Ching faced him and Mr. Leventine across the table. John had not asked him to sit down. Babu Ram Sen was at his desk in the corner and, "Sen," ordered John, "take down everything Mr. Ah Lee says. I want a typed report." Mr. Ah Lee! not Ching! Ching had seen John Quillan angry but never like this; he was dark with fury and as hard as if he were made of ice or stone. As for Mr. Leventine, he looked like a bewildered baby. "But it can't be," he kept saying. "A horse can't *vanish*." The word was piteous. "You're sure you have asked *everyone*? In the stables . . ."

Silence still hung over the stables as if the men were stunned; only the Jemadar walked up and down giving his brief orders; only the horses were normal, each in its stall, except Dark Invader.

"You have asked everyone?"

"Yes." John was terse.

"The police?"

"Yes," even terser.

"I shall see the Inspector myself."

"Do." John's patience was getting short.

The baby face grew shrewd. "This must be a *plot*. Someone has something against me."

"Before we jump to conclusions, suppose you listen to what Ching says." Ah Lee was Ching again, to his relief. "Tell Mr. Leventine exactly what happened –

from the beginning," said John.

Ching stood stiffly, trying not to betray his dismay – and his shame: it is part of Chinese manners to appear cheerful in disaster – and, "I extremely sorry, sir," he told Mr. Leventine, "I make so unhappy mistake . . ." he tried to laugh – a sound like 'Hee hee hee' – "but I think not all my fault."

"Of course it was your fault." John's temper snapped and Ching's small black Chinese eyes looked this way and that, trying to escape and, "Look at us, man," thundered John.

Ching looked and there was such distress behind the façade that John had to be gentle. "Try and tell us. Begin at the beginning."

"When Ted – Mr. Ted – Mr. Mullins – didn't . . ."

"Didn't appear – and obviously couldn't," John helped because Ching's voice had faded away from embarrassment. "Yes?"

"Jemadar Sahib and I, we not know what to do except horses must go out." John nodded in approval. "Then Sadiq tell us your list of orders, sir, orders for morning, was on table by bed – Ted's – Mr. Mullin's bed. Sadiq, he no want to fetch them, so. . . ."

"Who fetched them?"

"I, Ching," and Ching shut his eyes as if to shut out the memory of Ted's room. "Jemadar Sahib not read English, so I read . . . hoping that was right, sir?" It was a question and, "*That* was right," said John. "And we decide I take Mr. Ted's place, first riding boy take mine, etcetera, etcetera . . ." Ching was proud of that word. "Jemadar do timing. Was that right, sir?"

"*That* was right," said John again.

"I take Dark Invader. Not easy crossing road – so many peoples, but I take Ali with Sadiq, one each side. Then I do what you said: one, two circuits, like Mr. Ted. Then . . ." and Ching gulped.

"Then?"

"When we came back there was English jockeys, five, six, standing watching. When Darkie come in they all look at him. Me, I feel proud it is I, Ching, am riding him, and one of them say, 'Look. That the horse we got to beat for Viceroy Cup on Boxing Day. Never headed this season,' he say. I *very* proud," said Ching. "I go back to Jemadar and tell him.

"Then two jockeys, they come over and I knew one, sir. Him the famous Tom Bacon. I seen his photo . . . now he going round pretending he no had a ride. 'Want any work ridden?' he say. 'No?' He laugh. 'Very well, I push on,' he say, and, I," Ching swallowed, "I not understand he pretending . . . and he come up to me . . . I . . . pleased. English jockeys not speak much to us. He ask, 'You in charge here?'

"I say, 'This morning, yes.' Then I ask, 'Is Mr. Bacon?' and say, 'I seen your photo.'

"The other jockey, he laugh. He say, 'That's fame for you, Streaky!' Then Mr. Bacon look at Darkie and he say, 'Fine horse,' and other man – I think he not like Mr. Bacon very much – he say, 'Come off it, Streaky. It's Dark Invader. You've ridden him.'

"Mr. Bacon he say, 'Yes, I remember. Come to think of it I ride him his first race. Lingfield it was. We won *as* expected.'

"'You rode him again.'

"'Did I?' And Mr. Bacon say, 'I don't remember.'

142

"'You do! Doncaster,'" and, "Is that right name?" asked Ching. John nodded. "Other jockey, he go on, 'Sort of rode him, you mean. By all account he dumped you and ran home,' and Mr. Bacon, 'Really? I forgotten,' and, 'You know, Willie,' – Willie other man's name – 'You must allow for a jerk or two,' – I think he mean a fall," said Ching – "'in two year old race' and Mr. Willie, he say, 'Didn't look like a youngster's job. I behind you all the way. It look as if that horse he hate your guts.'

"Then Mr. Bacon he get angry." Ching's voice grew dramatic. "He say, 'I no having that sort of talk. Never been a horse that didn't take to me.' Then . . ."

"Then?" asked John.

"He laugh up at me, so nice like and say, 'Want any work ridden?' like to the others, and I told you I no understand he pretending, so I say . . ." Ching choked.

"Say?" John prompted him.

"I say 'Would be an honour, sir.' He say, 'Very well, I just take him round for you,' so I dismount, sir. He say, 'Why you ride so long? That old-fashioned.'" Ching gave a reproachful look at John. "What can I say but 'Is orders.' He laugh, say, 'Like ruddy mounted policeman,' and he shorten leathers, five holes. Then he take reins and I . . . I put him up. Mr. Willie say, 'Streaky, look out,' but Mr. Bacon no listening. He tell me, 'Thank you, chum.' 'Chum', like we was friend, so . . ."

"You let him go," said John.

"Yes. Hee hee . . ." Ching gave another nervous laugh.

"Go on," John was remorseless.

"I think Darkie – he taken by surprise. Because Sadiq and me, we holding him, he trust." Ching swallowed again.

"Go on."

"Mr. Willie shout again, 'Look out!' because, soon as the Streaky was in saddle, Darkie, he put back his ears; his eyes was like I never seen them. Streaky gather up the reins and Darkie – he go *puggle* – mad . . ." Ching shuddered. "Other English jockeys they was watching, laughing like it was a joke but Darkie almost standing on his head, then rearing . . . They laugh and shout, 'Where your magic, Streaky? *That* horse don't take to you!' and Mr. Bacon no like and as Darkie come up again, he so angry he give Darkie hard cut with his whip, wicked cut," said Ching. "Cross quarters and down below. Wicked cut – and Darkie make a neigh, high, like I never heard . . . he threw the Streaky backwards. Then just bolt. Quick I take Flashlight from the syce and go after – Jemadar send riding boy other way. I see nothing – only traffic roaring down Chowringhee . . . side road empty . . . I look, I ask . . . at last come back. Streaky Bacon, I think he stunned. They take him back to stands. I think he not forgive."

"Nor will we," said John.

VI

"Mother, are we going to try Beauty in the cart this evening?" Dark Invader had been re-christened Beauty. "Tonight?"

"Don't be simple, child. He's a racehorse," and, "I think perhaps a famous racehorse," Mother Morag might have added. "If we put him in the shafts, he would kick the cart to pieces."

"Then . . ." Elation went out of Sister Mary Fanny, "then he's no use to us."

"We'll see." Mother Morag would not say any more, but smiled her most enigmatic smile, a happy one, but as if she were secretly amused.

Sister Ignatius said much the same as Sister Mary Fanny but in her acid way. "One mustn't criticise the Almighty, I know, but while He was about it, He might have sent us a suitable horse."

"Perhaps He means us to use our wits."

"But, meanwhile, what are we going to do with it?" asked Sister Ignatius.

"If possible, nothing at all for twenty-four hours," said Mother Morag. "That will heighten the tension."

Certain measures, though, had to be taken. A track was marked out at the edge of the vegetable garden and three times a day Beauty was to walk "round and round it at least twenty times. If Gulab is too afraid I will attend to that myself, or Sister Joanna can," said Mother Morag. "She used to hunt." Gulab was overcome with pride at the monster now in his charge, but equally terrified. "I shall have to help groom," Mother Morag had a sparkle in her eyes; Gulab was too old to use the 'hart molesh' and, later that morning, the Community was edified to see their Superior working with him, brushing the brown coat, combing out the mane and tail with her fingers, sponging eyes and nose clean, and picking out the big feet while Gulab held them up. She even, and skilfully, bandaged the tail, "with our widest crêpe bandage," mourned Sister Anne, the infirmarian. Three times that day, in her black cloak, Mother Morag led the great horse round and round the vegetable garden, talking to him. "What do you talk about?" asked the Sisters.

"I say my prayers or the psalms. Beauty seemed to like it." Walking suited his laziness, just as the piece of bread and salt given as a prize for good conduct at the end suited his greed.

There were, though, other problems not as easily solved. "He must be properly rugged tonight," said Mother Morag. "Solomon's blankets are not thick enough. Nor are ours." They pondered until, "I know," said Mother Morag. "The quilt off the Bishop's bed."

The bed was not really the Bishop's – a bishop had only stayed with the Sisters once – but there was one room kept ready for visitors, "who are not accustomed to our ways." It was seldom used. "But

Mother," Sister Ignatius protested. "That quilt came to us from Belgium. It's handmade patchwork."

"It's warm. If that horse gets a chill . . ." and, for the rest of the day, Sister Ignatius went about, murmuring, "The Bishop's quilt! The Bishop's quilt!"

Another problem was food. "If I issue three or four times what we gave poor Solomon . . ." Sister Emmanuel, who was the cellarer, said.

"The horse will die of indigestion." The 'worry' line wiped out Mother Morag's smile.

"We haven't the money for corn or oats or whatever they have."

"No, we can't buy them," said Mother Morag. "But we could 'collect' them." The worry line was gone as, "Bunny," said Mother Morag.

"A miracle!" Bunny was ecstatic. Mother Morag confessed to Sister Ignatius that she had 'dressed' the story up a little for him and, like Sister Mary Fanny, he was quite sure it was a miracle. "And you are asking me to take part – to take part in a miracle! Thank you, Mother Morag. Thank you."

"You haven't heard what we want you to do yet."

"Anything. Anything."

"To begin with, we want to 'collect' from you."

"But," Bunny was dashed. "I haven't any money."

As he was not yet twenty-one, and as impetuous as he was extravagant, Bunny was under the strict control of a Resident appointed by the Government, "my Grey Eminence", as Bunny called him as irreverently as he called the British Government P.P. for

Paramount Power. "You know how tight they keep me." Only let you live in two palaces, go to London and the Riviera and play polo in India and England with a string of magnificent ponies, thought Mother Morag. "I could lend you an elephant, but that wouldn't help." Mother Morag thought of the elephant lumbering with the Sisters and the canisters from restaurant to restaurant and laughed. "I know I am ridiculous," said Bunny. Then his face brightened. "Jewels! I have some of my own from my Mother. They don't belong to the State. I could give you those."

"Dear Bunny – but nothing like that. Not jewels. Horse food."

"Horse food?"

"Yes, the very best, Your Highness." Now and again, Mother Morag reminded Bunny of his title. "We don't want this horse to suffer in any way. Solomon did very well on what Sister Emmanuel buys."

"What is that?"

"Mixed Horse Food, Grade Three: barley – sometimes there *are* weevils, split peas and lentils and rice-straw sweepings . . ."

"Ari bap!" said Bunny, "and he *lived*?"

"Solomon did but . . ." Mother Morag leaned across her desk – she was seeing Bunny in her office. "We need what you give your polo ponies and double that amount."

"I'll send you a lorry."

"No, no, Your Highness. Please no. Could you bring perhaps two sacks in the boot of your car?"

"I see." Bunny's eyes sparkled as Mother Morag's had done. "I am sworn to secrecy."

"Yes." The more sensational I am, the better, thought Mother Morag.

"I will do it now."

"And, for the moment, Your Highness will be discreet?"

Bunny's pride in all its Rajput royalty was offended. "My ancestors would cut out the tongues of anyone they thought might betray them. You have no need to do that to me."

"Bunny, I wouldn't think of cutting out your tongue." Mother Morag, who had risen, laid an affectionate hand on his shoulder. "Just – thank you and bless you."

Bunny brought the sacks. Dil Bahadur opened the gates to let him in and quickly closed them again. Mother Morag was in the courtyard to see them stored and then Bunny saw Dark Invader. "By God!" he said, then blushed. "I beg your pardon, Mother, but I can't wait to see Leventine's face."

"Leventine?"

"He's the owner, Mr. Casimir Alaric Bruce Leventine, and I think John Quillan will murder you for this. What fun!"

"I'm afraid he'll want to – but . . . one thing more," Mother Morag was serious. "Your Highness knows the people think our Convent is a place of sanctuary."

"Indeed yes," said Bunny. "It is a holy place."

"We try never to send anyone in distress away. This horse was terribly distressed. He was lathered. He had been beaten. Would you take a look at this."

Dark Invader looked anything but distressed but the weal from Streaky Bacon's whip still showed; as Bunny bent down to look further, the disingenuousness left him and he spoke as a horseman. "That's a vicious cut. There's blood on the sheath. You must call Captain Mack."

"I'm afraid so." The regret in Mother Morag's tone made Bunny look up at her. "I think you want me to do something. What do you want me to do?"

"As we can't keep it secret any longer, spread the news. How Beauty, as we call him, was lathered and beaten. How he took sanctuary here. You know how the people follow you."

That was true. Bunny had only to appear on the polo ground and the crowd hailed him. At the end of the game they pressed round to try and kiss his boots, his gloves, his polo stick, even his pony.

"I shall indeed spread it," said Bunny. "Far and wide."

Captain Mack usually drove in through the Convent gates to the courtyard, but now, to his surprise, they were closed and Dil Bahadur, who was watching for him, took him round to the front door which Captain Mack did not remember having used before. A Sister opened it and asked him to come upstairs, "to the Reverend Mother's office," where he found Mother Morag.

"This is unusually formal," he said.

"It's an unusual occasion. Captain Mack, will you

look out of the window and tell me if you see what I think I see?"

Captain Mack obediently looked and, "Holy mackerel!" he said.

Below him, loose in the yard, an unmistakable big brown horse was holding court – no other word for it. Sister Barbara and two other nuns were standing in a semi-circle and he moved gravely to each in turn, nuzzling hopefully, while they gave him bread and salt filched from the refectory. Gulab, who was beginning to overcome his awe, was wisping his flanks with a handful of straw – the Captain winced at the sight; tickling him like that was the surest way to get one of the nuns bitten – but the Invader paid no attention to what was happening to his short ribs. He was far too busy making friends and eating all that came his way. "Greedy old devil, always was," said Captain Mack. "Even ate his bedding."

"I hope he doesn't eat Solomon's, but Captain, that is Dark Invader, isn't it?"

The rich brown coat with the dark dapple, the obvious size and strength, the loose, almost lop, ears and the placid incurably friendly disposition seemed to give only one answer. "It certainly is, but who on earth brought him here?"

"No-one on earth – that's what my Sisters think. You see, we had no means of replacing Solomon, but we prayed." Mother Morag raised her expressive hands. "In fact, we were in Chapel when we heard the sound of his hooves."

"Extraordinary!"

"Not at all. It often happens to us."

151

"You mean the horse came of its own accord?"

"Seemingly so. He was alone, but saddled and bridled. He must have thrown his rider. I sent Dil Bahadur to look but there was no-one. My Sisters think the horse was looking . . ."

"Looking?"

"For sanctuary," and she said what she had said to Bunny, but more quietly. "Captain Mack, he was lathered, distressed – and marked."

"Couldn't have been." The Captain did not mean to be rude, but, "He was one of John Quillan's."

"Would you come and look. I had hoped to wait twenty-four hours, but Bunny said . . ."

"Bunny! Is he involved in this?"

"Indeed yes, thank heaven."

Feeling utterly bemused, Captain Mack followed Mother Morag down to the stable. "What do you say to that?" she asked when he had examined the cut.

Captain Mack looked up, his eyes dark with anger. "Someone must indeed have lost his temper and that wouldn't have been Ted Mullins, Darkie's jockey, nor any of the Quillan riding boys. Mysteriouser and mysteriouser," said Captain Mack.

He sent Dil Bahadur for his bag, gently cleaned the wound and handed Gulab a bottle of lotion. "Should be all right, but he must have exercise."

"He does. I and Sister Joanna do it ourselves." Mother Morag showed him the vegetable garden track and Captain Mack's lips twitched as he thought of the nuns in their habits walking the great horse round and round. They twitched still more when he saw Gulab rugging the Invader up with the Bishop's quilt under Solomon's old green blanket. Solomon's surcingle would not go round the Invader, so the nuns had had to lengthen it with some more of their precious crêpe bandages. "Really you deserve to succeed," said Captain Mack.

"Then you think it's all right?"

"I wouldn't interfere with you for the world," said Captain Mack, "but, all the same . . ."

"All the same?"

"You know what Dark Invader is?"

"I know."

"Favourite for the Viceroy's Cup."

"Which is fortunate for us."

"Backed to win lakhs of rupees."

Mother Morag's face, for a moment, seemed visionary. "Of which a few might come to us, rupees, not lakhs, I mean."

"Mother Morag. Wake up." The Captain had to say it. "Reverend Mother, as Veterinary Surgeon to the Turf Club, I am bound to tell the horse's owner where he is."

"Exactly what I want you to do," said Mother Morag.

Outside Captain Mack found Dil Bahadur. The little Gurkha was overflowing with gratification and pride. "You have seen our horse?" He and Captain Mack spoke in Nepali.

"Yes – how did he come here?" Captain Mack was stern. "Straight now."

"God sent him."

153

"Why?"

"Because we prayed." Dil Bahadur was astounded anyone could doubt it. "The Sister Sahibs. The Father. Gulab went to the temple. I to my Pujari and did a big puja for five rupees and when I got back the horse was here."

"Holy mackerel!" said the Captain again. "Four aces and the joker!"

The Captain's servant cranked the old Ford and the Captain took the wheel. There was a loud report and the car shot backwards as the Ford Model T was prone to do. "Hold up!" roared Captain Mack as to a stumbling horse, stamping on the pedals. He drove down the road and, as he went, suddenly began to laugh.

In the late afternoon Mr. Leventine, John Quillan and Ram Sen were in the office again after a fruitless search and, "Who knows about this?" asked Mr. Leventine.

"The whole stable, of course."

"I mean the people who matter."

"In a case like this everyone matters more than you think," John wanted to say but refrained. It was no use adding to the misery, and aloud he said, "You mean this evening's parade? I shall say we have sent Darkie to Barrackpore with – Ted." John could hardly bring himself to say the name. "Because of the crowds."

"Good. What about Bacon?"

"Streaky's the last person to talk about a fall – but the others? It's a matter of time and, anyway, when we

154

have found Darkie, will he be fit to run?"

"A rumour that he won't would mean a better price, then everyone will be suspicious. I cannot, I will not, countenance anything like that."

"It may be you'll have to." Again John did not say it and, He's thinking of his precious stewardship, thought John, of shaking hands with the Viceroy . . . but Mr. Leventine pounded his fist on the desk. "Let us get this clear. Until the facts are known, there must be no leakage to the Press or to anyone else. You hear me?" He hectored the babu.

"I think you are not speaking to me, sir," said Ram Sen with dignity and, "Then explain to me," said John, "how you can start to find a horse when you are forbidden to say that you have lost it?"

"Not *it* – my *horse*." Tempers were getting frayed and, "It's a plot," cried Mr. Leventine again. "Someone is jealous. One of you must have been bought." He was, mercifully, interrupted by the arrival of a car, the unmistakable bang and rattle of an old Ford T, and the sound of the bandar-log running to meet it, but Captain Mack, with his accustomed expertise, had got rid of them – probably he had a litter of puppies or rabbits in his car – because he appeared alone in the doorway. "Good afternoon – or should I say evening." He looked down at them all. "Och, man!" he said to Mr. Leventine. "You do look depressed. Is it possible you have lost a little something?"

Mr. Leventine sat upright in his chair. John lifted his head.

"A valuable little something?"

"Sandy, don't tease."

"I'm not teasing."

"You have found him?" Mr. Leventine jumped up.

"Not found. I was called in to him."

"Then he is injured?"

"Had a cut with a whip, but he's quite all right – in fact, in clover."

"Clover? Where is Clover?"

"Captain Mack means he is being well looked after. Stop clowning, Sandy," John said irritably. "Where is he?"

"In the Convent of the Sisters of Poverty just down the road."

"The *Convent*!" They both stared incredulously at Captain Mack. Then, "In God's name, how did he get there?" asked John.

"In God's name, precisely. That's what the Sisters believe," but Mr. Leventine was at the door.

"I will go and fetch him *immediately*. Johnny, call Sadiq and Ali," but, "Wait a minute," said Captain Mack.

"For what?"

"By a strange coincidence," said Captain Mack, "last night the Sisters lost their only means of transport. The horse that pulled their cart."

"What has that to do with this?"

"It would seem everything. If you knew your psalms, Mr. Leventine," the Captain was enjoying himself, "you would remember an inconvenient little set of verses," and he quoted: "Every beast is mine, the cattle upon a thousand hills. I know all the fowls of the mountain. The wild beasts of the field are mine. For the world is mine and the fulness thereof" which, of course, includes Dark Invader. Those verses are favourites of mine," said Captain Mack. "When I get sickened by the cruelty and indifference, I find them reassuring."

Mr. Leventine did not. "Poppycock," he said, a word he had learnt from Sir Humphrey.

"The nuns don't think it poppycock. They believe it." Captain Mack quoted again: "'Every beast is mine, and He, God, disposes.' I, unfortunately, had to put the Sisters' horse down. They had been praying for another and – hey presto!"

"That's enough of this!"

"Wait, Mr. Leventine," said Captain Mack. 'It's not only that. The Sisters believe Dark Invader took sanctuary with them."

"Sanctuary?"

"Yes – a refuge. A holy place where a fugitive, a runaway is safe from being taken away. Of course, that *can* be arranged," said Captain Mack, "but there must be conditions."

"I'll give them conditions! John, order the men."

"Look, Cas." For once John used the detested nickname. "This may be a ticklish situation. The Sisters have great influence. I know Mother Morag, their Superior. Let me go."

"It's my horse. Do as you're told."

The chauffeur cranked the car, the engine fired, the snake horn blared; children, hens, dogs scattered as the Minerva set off.

Never had the Convent front door bell been pulled as hard. It was followed too by a fusillade of knocks, but the portress, in her clean white apron, seemed unflustered. "Yes, sir?" she asked.

"I want to see the . . ." Mr. Leventine suddenly did not know what to call her. "The nun in charge – at once."

"I'm afraid it can't be at once," said Sister Bridget. "Reverend Mother is at Vespers."

"Vespers?" Mr. Leventine made it sound like an affront.

"Our evening prayer. Will you wait in the parlour?" and Mr. Leventine found himself penned, willy-nilly, in a small bare room, spotless from its plain stone floor to its whitewashed walls and ceiling, and furnished only with a table, wooden chairs, a small bookcase of books, its legs set in saucers of Jeyes Fluid against white ants, and a crucifix.

Twice Mr. Leventine rang the bell, twice the portress came. "Isn't this – what-d'you-call-it – over yet?"

"Not yet. They are listening to the reading now."

"But . . . this is interminable."

"Half an hour. That is not much."

The second time – "It will not be long. They are singing the Magnificat."

"The Magnificat?"

"Our Lady's song of praise and thanksgiving." The portress broke into a smile. "That has a special meaning for us today. We have been given a horse."

"Given!" Mr. Leventine did not ring the bell again.

*

"So you refuse to give him back."

"Under present conditions, yes, and I should have to think very carefully before something made me change my mind." For a moment the hazel eyes looked down. It was difficult for Mother Morag to keep a spice of amusement out of them, but she knew she must control them and look directly and seriously at Mr. Leventine, and she raised them again. "I might even have to consult our Mother General in Bruges."

"Bruges! That's in Belgium! Madam! The horse is due to race in five days."

"What a disappointment for you," said Mother Morag.

Mr. Leventine seemed to swell. "Madam, I am not accustomed to being disappointed."

"What an exceptional person you must be," said the cool voice.

"I am going straight to the Police, to Lall Bazaar."

Mother Morag inclined her head in acquiescence. "Then I will not keep you," she said.

In the railed red brick building of the Police Head-quarters in Lall Bazaar, the Chief Commissioner looked dispassionately at Mr. Leventine. He had been on the point of going home when his Deputy had come imploring him, "Chief, I cannot deal with this case. So much bluster," and he had handed over his notebook.

Now, under the Chief's bland considering gaze, even Mr. Leventine faltered and the blustering grew quieter, but still, "No action. No response," cried Mr.

Leventine. "Good God, Mr. Commissioner! My horse has been stolen."

"I think the Sisters of Poverty don't steal." The Commissioner had the notebook in front of him, but he asked another question or two. Then, "I am sorry," he said, "but for the moment it is better we do nothing. Police do not, on principle, interfere with religious premises or disputes."

"This is not a dispute. It is a fact . . . a *fact*."

"Disputes," the Commissioner went on as if he had not heard. "Hindu, Muslim, Buddhist, Christian – unless there is violence, and I find no violence here. The Sisters of Poverty are the most deserving of all charities. We know because we often send them the destitutes we pick up from the streets or gutters and old people who have been living in hovels. I expect you have passed them thousands of times – on the other side." Mr. Leventine drew his breath in sharply. Why should he, the injured party, be preached at? First Captain Mack, now this officer who was going on, "They do this city a great service and ask nothing in return."

"Except my most valuable horse."

"Not for themselves, Mr. Leventine. For you, to lose that horse means you forfeit the chance of winning perhaps a great deal of money and prestige. For them the loss of theirs spells hunger, not just for themselves, but for the two hundred or so people in their Home and, if I know them, many more. Have you ever been hungry, Mr. Leventine? I don't think so. Of course you can, if you wish, involve the law, but it will bring you a great deal of odium – also it will take time."

"Time! The race is in five days! No, it is almost four."

"Then I strongly advise you to settle with the Sisters yourself. Good evening, Mr. Leventine."

After Mr. Leventine had gone even more quietly than he came, the Commissioner, smiling more than a little, pulled a writing pad towards him. "Dear Reverend Mother," he wrote, "I have just seen Mr. Leventine and this is to tell you I endorse . . ."

Mother Morag did not open the letter until the next morning. By the time it had arrived, the Sisters were saying Compline, after which no outside business was allowed, no letters or even telephone calls, except in an emergency. "This is an emergency," she could imagine Mr. Leventine saying. "Not to us," she would have replied. The telephone had sounded angrily two or three times. There had also been a hammering on the front door and, in spite of her calm, Mother Morag had passed another sleepless night. "So how glad I was to have your note!" she wrote to the Commissioner.

Two tikka gharries had had to be hired for the night round. "We dare not let the collecting drop."

"But Mother, the expense!"

"It won't be for long," "I hope and pray," she added secretly. Though Mother Morag seemed completely in command, confident and serene, inwardly she was in turmoil, most of all because, "Is what I am doing right?" She would have given worlds to be able to talk to Father Joseph, but he was a timid man; worlds to

have consulted her Mother Provincial and Council
. . . what will they say to me, she thought.

After the canisters had been carried in, the food put
away, again she went into the chapel which was in
darkness, except for the glow of the tabernacle light.
That was steady and, "I must be steady too," she told
herself, but she was too tired to pray except for what
perhaps is the best prayer of all, to be still, not thinking of the price of tikka gharries or crushed oats or
tan-bark bedding: of Mr. Leventine or Bunny or John
Quillan – poor John, will he ever speak to me again?
Not thinking of Solomon or Dark Invader, not even of
the Sisters. Nothing – only, "Lord, Lord help me.
Help me to do what is right under the circumstances.
Lord."

Then, as dawn broke, she heard a bird singing and
went to the window; the Convent garden was still in
darkness but there was light in the sky and she could
just see the bird on the Convent gable end; it was a
magpie-robin boldly marking its territory before the
other birds began to sing, and she knew that the lovely
liquid melody was her answer; it was not only prayer, a
paean of praise, but defiance; not thanksgiving, but
aggression. What I have I hold for my nest, my helpless ones, and, "Thank you," said Mother Morag and
knelt down again.

Mr. Leventine was beside himself with fury and frus-
tration. "That Mother Morag! That nun!" Yet, suddenly, he seemed to see her again; the dignity with
which she held herself, the clear bones of her face, the

hazel eyes, delicate eyebrows; her hands – Mr. Leventine had not only a quick eye but, in a way, a connoisseur's one and, She must have been a beautiful girl, he thought illogically – appreciation does not generally mix with anger – and he was furious.

"If it wasn't for the Viceroy's Cup, I would let them keep the horse. That would teach them a damn good lesson. Let them try putting Darkie in between the shafts. If it wasn't for the Cup . . ."

"But there is the Cup," said John.

"I know." Mr. Leventine's voice rose almost to a shriek. "Johnny, you must get me out of this, you must."

Only you can do that, thought John and, aloud, "I asked you to let me see Mother Morag in the first place. Now . . ."

"I know, I know. But – each day that horse will be going down."

"I don't think so. Captain Mack . . ."

"From all I hear, those women could never afford to feed him."

"They can't. The food is being given by Bunny Malwa."

"The young Maharajah! *That* young reprobate?"

"He is a great friend of Mother Morag's."

"But . . ." Mr. Leventine was getting more and more bewildered. "I thought nuns were saintly people."

"I think you'll find that saints never minded whom they mixed with. It's the rest of us who do that," but John was getting weary. "All right," he said. "I'll try."

*

163

"A horse forced to race against its will," – from the bandar-log Mother Morag had heard every detail of Dark Invader's dramatic story – "ridden by a jockey it dreaded. Who knows what pain he once inflicted? Handed over to him again by your man and, when it refused, given the cruellest of cuts – ask Captain Mack, or I'll show you myself – bolted blind with fear and pain. . . ."

"Have you finished?" asked John.

"I see I needn't go on." Mother Morag smiled. "You're quite right. I knew it was a chain of seeming accidents."

"Seeming?"

"Yes, I said 'seeming', but that is the story and it will spread as long as Dark Invader is here."

"Which is to your advantage."

"Of course. Also, we Sisters of Poverty take an extra vow as well as the usual three; it is the vow of hospitality. We cannot turn anyone in distress away – not even a horse." John could have sworn there was a mischievous glint in her eyes. "And do you know, Mr. Quillan, that yesterday happened to be December 21st, St Thomas's Day, when anyone in need has the right to ask alms?"

"Mother Morag!"

"It is true." Now the eyes were candid, innocent.

"We could get an injunction."

"I doubt it. I had a letter from the Commissioner of Police this morning."

"So you have him in your pocket too."

She ignored that and went on. "In any case, if you succeeded, I doubt if the crowds would let you get

Dark Invader to the racecourse. You know what mobs are, particularly Indian ones. Your stables might be invaded. Mr. Leventine's beautiful car might be stoned. There could be a riot."

"Are you spinning me another tale?"

"This time not. There has already been an encounter between two of your men, the syces who came with Mr. Leventine for Dark Invader, them and our gateman."

Dil Bahadur had spoken to Sadiq and Ali first through a grating in the gates. "What do you want?"

"We have come to fetch our horse."

"*Our* horse," contradicted Dil Bahadur.

"Ours!"

Dil Bahadur opened the wicket and came out on to the pavement, closing the door behind him.

They had confronted one another, the two Muslims – Sadiq's upturned moustaches were fierce – and the little brown man in a starched drill tunic and medals, which included the Indian Distinguished Service Medal and three chevrons. A pillbox hat in black velvet cut in patterns sat firmly over one ear and his shaven skull, criss-crossed with the scars and weals of old wounds, gleamed in the evening sun. Dil Bahadur's face, which could be so genial, was wiped clean of all humour. His mouth was a thin line, his eyes like brown stones. "You will not enter. No one will enter. It is the Mother Sahib's orders. I, Dil Bahadur, say so. You see these medals? With this kukri I, Dil Bahadur, cut off the heads of eight Germans." He made an expressive gesture and held up his fingers, "Eight – and, if you do not go away, I

165

will cut off your heads too. It would not be difficult. Go away." He began to crowd them along the wall. "This is a holy place," said Dil Bahadur.

"Which is what saved the situation," said Mother Morag now, "but two Muslims and a Gurkha, that's dangerous and you know how inflammable the people are. It only needs a little agitation."

"Which you will provide?" John was still angry.

"We?" The eyebrows lifted. "I am doing my best to prevent it. It's not I who can start or stop it."

"Then who. . . ?"

"Mr. Leventine."

"And if he won't move?"

"A little pressure from Bunny . . ."

John had forgotten Bunny and his power, how he had only to speak or lift a finger. Against Bunny, Mr. Leventine would not have a chance, and, "You may be a nun," said John, "but you are a devilishly clever woman."

"Not devilish, I hope, and certainly not clever, though I grant we are adept in begging. Not an easy thing to learn," said Mother Morag, "especially if you are born proud but, if you believe it gives people the chance . . ."

"The chance?"

"To become Providence, which is of God," and Mother Morag bent her head. Her hands were on her desk – beautiful hands, Mr. Leventine had thought, but John noticed how toil-worn they were – held together now in the attitude of prayer – the same, he suddenly thought, as the Indian greeting of reverence, namaskar. What he did not see was that their tips were

166

tightly pressed together. Then she gave a smile that was tender. "Yes, Bunny," she said. "Fortunately His Highness believes in miracles."

"So that's what they are beginning to call this!"

"Yes."

"But you?" John was astute.

Mother Morag smiled again. "What most people, shall we say in the world, call miracles, are to us perfectly normal. We have a need – in this case, a horse – and, by God's providence, a horse was sent."

"Then your God doesn't know much about horses."

"His ways are certainly sometimes difficult to understand," she admitted. "He helps us, but we also have to help ourselves. Suppose you bring Mr. Leventine to see me again."

"He is outside, fuming."

"This is blackmail," said Mr. Leventine.

"Isn't it, rather, nemesis?" but that was another word Mr. Leventine did not know. "For thirty-five years," said Mother Morag, "first as a young Sister, then as Superior, I have helped to organise the collecting by which our old people live – scraps of food, Mr. Leventine, scraps of money to rich people like you. Our Sisters go round the offices and most firms are generous, but yours is one of the few where, every time, they get a rebuff. It seems Leventine and Son cannot afford to spare an anna."

"Afford!" That affronted Mr. Leventine. "Madam, we are one of the most successful firms of our size in the city."

167

Out of your own mouth, thought John – he was enjoying this.

"Then perhaps it really would take a miracle to change your heart?"

"I thought you said this was Providence," said John.

"Yes, but maybe something more. Usually one can find an explanation for Providence, but how do you explain, Mr. Quillan, when Dark Invader bolted, as I have heard he did, then turned and trotted, when his own stable was such a short way off, that he should suddenly have turned in here? Why?"

"I don't know," said John.

"Nobody knows, but I think we Sisters can guess. Well then?" said Mother Morag.

Mr. Leventine looked at her. He knew he was beaten. His heart, that Mother Morag had spoken of, also knew, under his ornate waistcoat, that it had had enough. His bewildered eyes were sharp again as he asked, "How much for Dark Invader?"

"Money?" The eyebrows went up. "Not money, Mr. Leventine. The people would never understand that. To them, though, one horse is much like another. If you would give us a carriage horse used to harness, strong yet tractable – our driver is not very skilled – a horse not too young but not too old," her voice faltered, she was thinking of Solomon. "One that Captain Mack and Mr. Quillan would approve . . ."

Mr. Leventine was affronted again. "Madam, I think you will find I am as good if not a better judge of a horse than they. *They* would not have bought Dark Invader."

"You have twenty-four hours," John told Mr. Leventine. "Today is the 22nd and I must have three days to get Dark Invader wound up." John had not tried to gain time – by now he knew Mother Morag too well – but Mr. Leventine had. "If I give you my promise."

"Promises won't do, Mr. Leventine. Think of the people. A horse can go, certainly, but there must be a horse here."

"I only hope," said Captain Mack, "that he doesn't think he can get away with rubbish, something that takes the eye. He's probably sure that a nun can't know one end of a horse from another."

"Let things take their course," said John and smiled.

That afternoon Mr. Leventine was outside the Convent, stamping his foot imperiously on the bell of a smart Cee spring buggy. In the shafts was a good looking bay horse, well-groomed and, by his appearance, English rather than Australian. Mr. Leventine pulled up, got down and waited with every satisfaction for Mother Morag to appear.

"Certainly rather good-looking," she said, which, by her tone, sounded derogatory, and she seemed, to Mr. Leventine's dismay, to take in the whole of the horse with one glance. She walked to its head, rubbed the nose and lifted the upper lip with a deft finger, then, "No thank you," said Mother Morag.

"No thank you?" Mr. Leventine was dazed.

"How can you, Mr. Leventine!" Mother Morag was stern. "You are wasting your time – and mine. This horse has been raced. At some time he has sprained a

169

tendon and the injury has calloused. That wouldn't interfere with his work, but I said, 'Not too young,' also 'not too old.' This horse is twenty."

"Madam, you must be mistaken."

"Perhaps I am; perhaps he is even older. Look at that corner tooth, Mr. Leventine. It will tell you his whole story, so – no thank you."

Mr. Leventine was chagrined, but challenged too. "Why not settle for that roan country-bred, Raj Kumar, belonging to the Nawab?" asked John. "I actually have him in the stable. No good for racing but broken to carriage work, strong, docile, six years old. Ideal. The Nawab would let you have him for a thousand rupees."

"A thousand! Five hundred is the price for a country-bred."

"He won't let it go for less," John shrugged. "Alright, go your own way, but remember, every hour is precious."

All the same, Mr. Leventine could not resist trying again. This time it was a dapple grey – "a colour ladies seem to like" – and a true carriage horse, belonging to a Greek, Mr. Petrides, who drove sedately to his office every morning, sedately back every evening, and was now retiring so that his Bimbo was for sale. Bimbo was ten years old, but had been little used – "an advantage in a car but not in a horse," said Mother Morag – and, "overfed, underworked and listen, Mr. Leventine," she lifted her arm in a sudden deliberate gesture so that her sleeve flapped, startling Bimbo into the loud grunt that spells a broken wind. This time Mother Morag had no need to speak to Mr.

Leventine or to say, "No thank you." She simply looked at him in reproach.

Mr. Leventine found himself with another curious new feeling. He was torn; half of him filled with chagrin because, for once, he could not make a bargain, half of him filled with admiration for this, to him, revelation of a nun.

"Cas, why not give in?" said John. "Take her the roan."

"But the price! A thousand rupees."

"I'll pay half," said John. "After all, the whole thing is my fault," but, for some reason he did not understand, Mr. Leventine refused. "Have I ever before refused to bargain?" He did not know what was the matter with him – it was like having teeth drawn – but an hour later he and the buggy drove into the Convent again, and this time, between the shafts was a horse, but one with a difference, an upstanding red-roan with the arched neck, corkscrew ears of an Indian country-bred, and a splendid Arab tail. He was strong, vigorous, but obviously tractable with an intelligent but docile eye and, "Ah!" said Mother Morag.

She examined him as carefully as she had the others, but this time her voice was warm, her eyes bright. Then, putting the last hoof down and giving the right flank a pat, she said, "I should like to try him."

"Try him. You mean . . ."

"I mean that while a horse may seem suitable, until he is ridden or driven . . ."

"I will take you gladly. Let me help you up," and, as

171

he joined her and Sister Ignatius in the buggy, "Now where shall I drive you?"

"I will drive." Mother Morag had already gathered up the reins. Mr. Leventine had never thought he would be seen being driven round Ballygunj in a buggy by a nun, another sitting up behind, but he soon forgot his embarrassment as he saw how Mother Morag drove, with what skill she coaxed response from the strong roan, how lightly she held him.

"But how," he was to ask John when he got back to the office, "how does a nun know about horses?"

"Simple," said Captain Mack – they were all gathered there – "she was born to it. Her father was Dawson – Rattler Dawson – the leading horse dealer in Dublin."

"Yes," said Bunny. "That's how I met her. My father used to buy horses from her father. He made a fortune from us because Papa wouldn't have any other colour than chestnut and didn't mind what he paid."

"And Mother Morag – Helen Dawson as she was then – used to show off hunters when she was still at school," said John. "I believe that did wonders with the young cavalry officers from the Curragh. Couldn't bear to be bested by a brat in pigtails," and he said, "she knows all right."

"She certainly knows," said Mr. Leventine gloomily.

"That *was* satisfactory," Mother Morag had said as she jumped down from the buggy. Mr. Leventine had been ready to help her, but she jumped down like a girl and he was left to help stiff old Sister Ignatius. "How I enjoyed that!" She sounded so elated that he was not prepared for what came next. "Of course we still have to try him in the cart."

"The . . . cart?"

"Yes – it's much more difficult than a beautifully sprung buggy. It's heavy and awkward. Also we must see if Gulab, our driver, can manage Raj Kumar who is not yet as well-trained as Solomon, but you'll see."

"You mean . . . I am to come with you?" This time Mr. Leventine really did shrink, but mysteriously found himself seated next to the driver in the cart. "This is what she does to you," Bunny was to tell him, "and you don't know how."

The cart did not run, it trundled; the tyres on its large wheels were so thin that it jarred. Its roof was of canvas so old that obviously it had let in the rain and it stank of mildew. The flooring was of rough planking on which some dozen canisters, as large as dustbins, rattled. The lights were two hand-lanterns that swung from hooks each side of the cart; another was hung inside. There were two small wooden seats for the Sisters while, in front, a wide plank set on battens and covered with a strip of carpet made the driver's seat, and, "This is impossible," said Mr. Leventine. He hoped, almost prayed, that nobody he knew would see him perched up beside the old Hindu bundled in his ancient coat. What if Sir Humphrey should pass? Mr. Leventine shrank back under the hood but still he felt conspicuous and, "Impossible," he said.

"It is what we have," Mother Morag was serene, "and has been possible for years. Would you believe it, Mr. Leventine, that this old cart has been the means of feeding some hundreds of people every day?" She did not add, "with what you throw away!" "But sometimes I do not know how Gulab manages it."

"Nor do I," said Mr. Leventine.

"It will be better with Strawberry," – the Sisters had already abandoned the grand name of Raj Kumar for homely Strawberry, and, "Strawberry is more adroit," said Mother Morag.

Back in the Convent courtyard she patted him gratefully. "Poor old Solomon's mouth was hard," and, "Better with Strawberry," she told Gulab who was already gleaming with pride.

"And better still," said Mr. Leventine, "you will have the buggy."

"The buggy?"

"The buggy, of course, is yours too."

That did take her by surprise. "But, dear Mr. Leventine, what should we do with a buggy? How would it hold our canisters? Protect the Sisters in wet weather? Yes, I know our canvas leaks, but . . ."

"You could use the buggy for errands," but she shook her head.

"The poor don't have buggies and we are Sisters of Poverty; we do our errands as they do, by 'bus or tram, or on our own feet when we can't afford fares. We have the cart only for our 'collecting' and Strawberry must pull that. It is most kind of you . . ." She paused, then a look came over her face, a shrewdness, twin, he recognised with unexpected comradeship, of his own. "Of course, as you are so generous, perhaps the cost of the buggy could repair our cart."

"Repair *that*! You shall have a new cart." Mr. Leventine seemed unable to stop himself saying it and at once wanted to retract. He should have added "one day," which would have meant never; he was just going to say it when the old Sister spoke, the one who had accompanied Mother Morag like a shadow and had never opened her mouth. Now, in a curiously deep and impressive voice, she said, "God bless you, Mr. Leventine," and a strange feeling of happiness that seemed to come from outside himself warmed and illumined Mr. Leventine. He had never been blessed before.

Strawberry's papers and certificates had been handed over, "Now all we have to do," said Mr. Leventine, "is make our amicable exchange," and another, even stranger, sensation filled him, a feeling of deep gratification, though why he should be gratified when he had been forced – yes, forced – to spend a great deal of money, he did not know, but he felt it, as he said, "our amicable exchange. The Quillan syces have arrived to fetch Dark Invader." He bowed to Mother Morag in what was meant to be a farewell, but a crowd had gathered outside the gate, a crowd that was growing larger; the air was full of murmurs and wonderings and Mother Morag said suddenly, "It would be wise – I think imperative – that the people see the horse goes willingly."

Dark Invader would not go willingly. After these two halcyon days, he had no intention of returning to the effort and stress of the racecourse. The quiet walks around the vegetable garden while he was talked to gently, or heard gentle talking – the fact that Mother Morag was saying a psalm made no difference to Dark Invader – the tidbits of bread and salt that came like manna from heaven at unexpected times, Gulab's and Mother Morag's gentle grooming, none of that thump and slapping, all suited his large, lazy and greedy self. When Gulab led him out of the stall he thought at first it was for another quiet wander or some more bread and salt. Instead, he saw Sadiq and Ali advancing. Dark Invader stopped, looking carefully, then laid back his ears, showed his teeth and, when Sadiq put his hand on the halter rope, taking it from Gulab, the Invader gave vent to a sideways swing of his head that hit his hard jawbone on Gulab's face and drew a gasp from the crowd.

Then they, Mr. Leventine and the nuns, were given a display of such horse fireworks they had never seen or imagined. Dark Invader kicked, reared, beating the air with his forefeet, bringing them down on the cobblestones with a crash and going up again. Sadiq and Ali manfully held on, dodging the flashing hoofs, shouting and cursing, while Mr. Leventine wailed, "Last time it was on the racecourse on grass, here it is stone. He will come down. He will injure himself." It was only the appearance of Sister Barbara and Sister Joanna bearing, like handmaidens, slices of bread and salt, calling in their cooing voices, "Beauty, Beauty, Beauty," that made Dark Invader stop. As if nothing had happened, he accepted their tidbits and when Sister Joanna took the rope from Sadiq, let her lead him towards the vegetable garden leaving the two grooms out of breath and shamed, their turbans half off their heads, and furiously, "Allah! Ismallah! Shaitan! Satan!" Sadiq muttered, rewinding his turban, while Gulab staunched his nosebleed. "Do you think," the shattered Mr. Leventine asked Mother Morag, "that the sight of Sadiq could have brought back this famous fear?"

"Not at all," said Mother Morag. "The horse was not sweating or lathered or trembling. He simply wanted to have his own way – but poor Sadiq and Gulab."

"Of course." Mr. Leventine slapped his thigh. "Of course, that fool Johnny should never have sent them," and he bellowed, "Why didn't he send Ted Mullins?" and Mr. Leventine ordered, "Telephone Quillan and tell him to send Mullins at once. No – wait," and Mr. Leventine said majestically, "I will fetch him myself."

"Mullins. *Mullins!*"

Ted raised his head. He was sitting where he had sat for most of the last two days – at the desk in the darkest corner of the darkened room – he had kept the shutters closed. There was nothing on the desk now; the photograph of him and Ella in her 'lace curtain' had been shut away in the drawer, as had been the framed form of his new licence. From long habit he had gone to bed at night, undressed, put on his nightshirt, only to lie awake; at dawn when he heard the Jemadar's call, he got up, shaved and dressed but, as he heard the horses go out, he took a cup of tea from Ahmed's tray, leaving the toast and bananas untouched, and shut himself in the room again. "He will die!" Dahlia wept in her distress. "For two days he has taken nothing but that cup of tea, no food, no drink. He will die."

"No one dies from going without food or drink for two days," said John.

"Papa – you must forgive poor Ted. You must." The bandar-log were frantic. "You are not to go near him," John had ordered them, but of course they disobeyed, or would have if Ted had allowed it, but, "If your Pa says no – no it is," Ted's voice had said from inside. Still they kept vigil, tried to prise open the shutters with their fingers, to creep in through the bathroom, but he had locked the inner door.

"Papa. *Please, please,*" but, "Mr. Mullins," John had said, "is going straight back to England."

"But John, why are you so hard?" Dahlia pleaded. "You're not usually so hard."

"Because usually I know what to expect, but I trusted Ted." There were few people John Quillan trusted and Dahlia knew he was not only angry but hurt, deeply hurt and, "I don't want to see him again," said John.

Ted knew it and shut himself out of sight. Now, "Mullins, open the door."

It was the voice of authority. Dazed, Ted got up, drew back the bolts and opened the shutters, wincing at the light.

"And what do you think you are doing? Or not doing?" asked Mr. Leventine.

"Doing?" mumbled Ted.

178

"Why are you not with your charge? With Dark Invader?"

"The . . . the Invader, sir?" Ted croaked. "I knew he had been found, thanks be. Mr. Quillan sent me a note." "I had to, in decency," John said. "But I thought . . . thought he was out of the race, that he wouldn't race now."

"And what business have you in thinking? Who says he's out of the race?"

"Then – he isn't?" Joy lit up Ted's face. "You mean he's fit! But . . ." and the shame came back. "Anyway, I'm out."

"Who says so?"

"Mr. Quillan."

"Who employs you?" Mr. Leventine's 'Who?'s grew more and more regal. "I – or Mr. Quillan?"

"I suppose . . . you do, sir."

"Exactly," said Mr. Leventine. "You will take your orders from me, and at this moment they are that you will come with me in my car and get this . . . this animal out of this ridiculous situation and bring him immediately home."

"Me?" Ted sounded as if he could not believe his ears.

"Who else?" and Mr. Leventine, looking down at the little man who seemed to have shrunk even more and aged by twenty years, put a plump hand on the rigid shoulder and said, "I think no one else but you can do it, Teddy."

Far from grating on him, the silly little nickname heartened Ted as nothing else could have done. No one since Ella had called him Teddy and Ted took his clean handkerchief out of his pocket – by habit he had a clean handkerchief every morning – used it, put it meticulously away and said, "I'm ready, sir."

"We call him Beauty," Sister Joanna told Ted and Ted's chivalry rose to the occasion. "A good name for him, ma'am."

"Not ma'am. I'm a Sister."

"Ain't never had a sister." It was an emotional evening for Ted, but that did not prevent him giving Dark Invader a thorough rating. "You shocker! That's what you are, a shocker."

A secret fear had been removed from Ted; he could not help remembering, even though he had been fuddled, how Dark Invader had not greeted him that night. "Thought he had gone off me for Mr. Saddick," but when Ted gave his whistle across the Convent vegetable garden, Dark Invader pricked his ears. There was a loud whicker of welcome and the Invader tried to break away from Gulab and Sister Joanna. Ted had gone quickly to the rescue. "Shocker! Putting it on for these kind ladies. Never heard of such a thing, but don't think you can get away with it. You've been too kind to him, ma'am – Sister," and, "You're coming home, my lad," said Ted to Dark Invader who looked at him lovingly, a cabbage-leaf dangling from his lips – nothing had been nicer than the nibbles of fresh vegetables in the Convent garden, but, "Home". Ted said it sternly and, recalling his war years, "Toot de sweet and the tooter the sweeter."

180

"But how do you think you'll get him there?" asked Sister Joanna.

"Ride him, of course. Would you ask that man of yours to bring the saddle and bridle?" My saddle, Ted almost said, Ching didn't ought to have touched it, but remembering the reason, blushed and kept quiet and was glad that he had when John Quillan appeared with Gulab. He did not speak to Ted but gave him a leg up when Dark Invader had been saddled and bridled; he had not objected even when Ted tightened the girth. "He's wise enough to know when the game's up," Ted told Sister Joanna. Once more in the saddle he gathered up the reins. "Say goodbye and thank you."

"But wouldn't it be safer," Sister Ignatius said, "if we opened the garden gate and he went out that way?"

"That wouldn't do," said Mother Morag. "He must leave through the crowd," and, "It will probably be *with* the crowd."

The crowd was getting bigger, they could hear the rising hum and, "Can you manage him?" asked anxious Mr. Leventine.

"Gawd Almighty!" said Ted; back in the saddle with Dark Invader under him, that was almost the power he felt. "The Invader and I, ain't we used to crowds?" and he ran his finger in the familiar Ted gesture up the long line of Dark Invader's mane, but there was a doubt in Ted's mind. John Quillan had given Ted his chance, almost equally with Mr. Leventine, gone along with him all the way and, though John now was silent, hostile, Ted was not taking Dark Invader out without his permission and, "Mr. Quillan, sir?" asked Ted. It was a beseeching.

John raised his head and perhaps only Dahlia could have told what the quirk of a smile he gave Ted meant, and, "Go to it, Ted," said John.

"Almost as big a crowd as for the Cup," said John.

There had been no trouble, no Invader antics. Mother Morag had pulled his ears and given him a most un-nun like slap on the rump. Sister Joanna had whispered, "We shall miss you, Beauty," and Ted had ridden him out of the vegetable garden, through the courtyard, past the rows of nuns, past Gulab who, with a swollen nose, was standing guard over the stable where Strawberry was eating his supper, past Dil Bahadur who saluted, and into the crowd which parted respectfully then, as Mother Morag had predicted, arranged itself to accompany them up the road. Bunny had driven up – "I thought it wise to ask him," said Mother Morag – and he controlled the concourse, but Ted sat easily, using the long rein. Only once did he jerk it when Dark Invader nosed too eagerly for the jilipis and sweets that were offered. Marigolds were thrown down too and both were garlanded. Dark Invader put his head down graciously as if flowers were his due, but Ted turned a deeper bronze and hunched his shoulders. Sadiq and Ali followed, chastened, and as they neared the Quillan stables, the bandar-log came dancing down, and, as Ted dismounted, Dahlia, who was waiting by

Dark Invader's stall, threw her arms round Ted's neck and kissed him.

"A little fast work tomorrow morning," John gave Ted his orders, as if nothing had happened, thought Ted. "You can take him as far as the four furlong mark. Ching can pace you with Flashlight. Repeat on Christmas Day, then, on the morning of the race, a two furlong sprint just to clear his wind. Got that?" asked John.

"Yes sir," said Ted.

Sir Humphrey met Mr. Leventine on Christmas Day in the billiard room where both had taken refuge – sanctuary, thought Mr. Leventine.

"Well, how are you, Leventine?"

"Thank you. I'm in clover."

"Hear you had some trouble with your horse down on the course."

"Just nemesis," Mr. Leventine waved his hand. "We were foolish enough to let another jockey try him."

"Doesn't answer so close to the race. Hope it hasn't impaired his chances."

"We still hope to turn a nimble shilling on him."

The Judge looked slightly astonished but only said, "Well, good wishes for the day."

"Bless you, Sir Humphrey," said Mr. Leventine.

*

The Sisters had made a small crib in the Chapel. "In the excitement I had almost forgotten tomorrow is Christmas Eve," and Dahlia brought the bandar-log to see it.

"Don't take them," said John. "They won't know what it means and will want to play with it and probably tear it to pieces."

They certainly knew what it meant. They had brought with them two small clay horses, one painted dark brown, the other dark red. "Mohan, our friend in the bazaar made them for us. Don't you think they're pretty?"

"Very pretty," said Mother Morag. Mohan, in the way of Indian potters, had added a few painted daisies and golden necklaces.

"They are to stand close to the Jesus," said the eldest boy.

"Oh no! they can't." Sister Ignatius was shocked.

"Why not? You have an ox and an ass."

"And they must. Darkie has come to say 'thank you'. Strawberry has come to say 'please'," explained the eldest girl.

"No – they have both come to say 'thank you'. They both have come to say 'please'," said the bandar who was the youngest except for the two babies. At that moment, with his big eyes turned up to look at Mother Morag, he looked less like a monkey, more like a wise little owl and, "Yes, put them close to the manger," said Mother Morag, and both of them shall say thank you *and* please, so shall we," and that night in chapel she announced, "Tonight we shall sing the Te Deum:"

THE DARK HORSE

Te Deum laudamus: te Dominum confitemur
Te aeternum patrem omnis terra veneratur

We praise thee, O God . . .
All the earth doth worship thee . . .

Dark Invader was back unharmed at Quillan's.
Strawberry was in the Convent stall. "Tonight we will
take him on the round, and I don't think we'll need
any more expensive tikka gharries," Mother Morag
told Sister Ignatius. Mr. Leventine had promised a
new cart. John Quillan was mollified, though Captain
Mack still smiled. Bunny was enchanted, but Mother
Morag's knees felt weak all the same and she said, "I
don't want to see or hear a magpie-robin again." Then
she stopped. "But – magpie-robins . . . they don't
come till March. That one I heard" – she almost said,
spoke to me – "was singing out of season!"

VII

The start of the Viceroy's Cup was in front of the stands which made it more of an ordeal for jockeys and the starter; the business of getting nervous spirited thoroughbreds into line needed not only skill, patience and immense authority, but unquestionable fairness.

It was the greatest day of the whole racing year. Flags flew over the stands, and banks of potted flowers filled every corner, dahlias in garish colours, chrysanthemums – white, yellow and gold – and the blue of cinerarias. No lawns were ever greener, no ropes and rails whiter, and the track itself stretched like a wide emerald ribbon in the golden sunlight of the Bengal winter.

The Governor had arrived in state; after him, in greater state, the Viceroy, both in four-horse landaus, shaded by scarlet and gold umbrellas, and accompanied by the Lancers, their horses matched, white sheepskins on their saddles, pennons flying below glittering lance points, jackboots, red coats, white breeches immaculate, and dark faces bearded under a pride of turbans, starched in blue and gold; the whole

186

noiseless on the grass, except for the clink of bits and chains and the creak of leather. There was a fanfare of trumpets in the royal salute while the Stewards stood in an array of grey morning suits, white carnations and white topees, which would presently be replaced by grey top hats.

The Members' Enclosure was filled; the women's dresses, hats and sunshades were worthy of Ascot or Longchamps but, for beauty and elegance, could not match the exquisite shimmering saris of the Indian women, nor the turbans of the visiting Princes. Bunny had a pink gauze one with an emerald in front, "Your colours," he told Mr. Leventine, "happiness and hope. I'm not allowed to bet," Bunny said ruefully – he had lost a small fortune on racecourses and in casinos before he was twenty, "but I would have put twenty thousand on your Invader."

"If the bookie would have taken it," said John.

"I could have put it on the Tote," but, "Don't be too sure yet," said Mr. Leventine. He was still superstitious and John added, "This *is* the crux – the first real test. Darkie won't be able to gallop away with it as he has so far – not with this lot."

It was time for the big race. The staircases were lined by the now dismounted Lancer bodyguards. There was no mistaking the importance of the occasion.

For the first time Ted was nervous. He had not been helped in the changing room. His stock would not come right; he pulled it off and gestured to the bearer for a new one. Then the jockeys who had ridden in the race before came in, unbuttoning their silks and putting on new colours, picking up saddles and weight cloths and taking turns on the scales, trying their weight. Among them were Streaky Bacon, Willie Hunt and three other English jockeys. Streaky paused when he saw Ted. "Hullo – here's Father Christmas."

"Methusaleh," said one of the others, but Streaky looked closer. "Seen you before. Weren't you one of Michael Traherne's strappers?" He straddled the floor. "And what are you doing here, may I ask?"

"Riding," Ted said briefly.

"Riding for Quillan, Mr. Leventine's Dark Invader," put in one of the others.

"Cor! The comeback of all time! Methuselah in person. Riding Dark Invader!"

"Which is more than you can do." Willie's voice came across the room, heartening Ted. "Remember Thursday morning," said Willie and Bacon turned away, but Ted saw him go into a huddle with his friends.

Ted had expected this. "Watch out for Bacon," John had said, but what Ted had not expected was the crawling feeling in his guts, the sudden cold sweat that broke out on his neck and hands. This was the first time Dark Invader had appeared since his encounter with Streaky. Ted was going to race with him and against him. Would there be trouble? Ted looked at the order on the race card. "Thank God I didn't draw next to him."

Ted fastened his silks, tucked them into his breeches, picked up his whip, saddle and weight cloth and went on to the scales for a final check.

They were singing at him now, a ribald version of 'John Anderson My Jo':

THE DARK HORSE

Now your brow is bald, Ted,
Your locks are like the snow,
But blessings on your frosty pow . . .
pow pow pow'

"Blessings! I don't think," said Streaky Bacon.

Ted could almost feel the grizzle among the fair tuft on his head. He tried not to hurry as he pulled on his cap. His legs felt so clamped with terror that he seemed to swagger as he walked. If only there had not been the bad luck of Streaky's appearance. If only Streaky had not got near Dark Invader. If only . . . He, Ted, had let John Quillan down. Would he let Mr. Leventine down – Mr. Leventine who had such trust in him? If . . . if . . . if. Then Ted remembered that Sister who had been leading Dark Invader. At parting she had said, "Oh, I do hope you'll win." Then she had caught herself back. "I suppose one mustn't pray for racing."

"Prob'ly not," Ted had said – he was not used to talking about praying, but in the strangeness of the Convent he had been led to add, "You can pray for the Invader and for me." Must have been out of meself, Ted had thought afterwards. What would Ella have said but, standing on the vegetable garden path, the young Sister had looked so appealing that, "If you will, my dear," Ted had said. The 'my dear' made it seem more paternalistic but, "Oh, I will. All of us will," she had said fervently and, "That's the way for us to win," Ted had said.

Now a little knot seemed to form inside Ted. "If you've got the jitters, whatever you do, don't pass them on to the Invader. He's going to need all he's got, so you forgets about your blinking self," Ted Mullins told Ted Mullins.

As the crowd watched, the first little brightly clad figures came through the door of the weighing room verandah and sat down on the bench. The judges in the Judges' Box identified them. Blue bird's eye, orange cap, that would be Quarterback, a grey five year old from Bombay. White, red sleeves, red cap – Backgammon, ridden by Streaky Bacon, the visiting crack brought out specially by the Rajah of Raniganj. Here was another, a chessboard effect, black and white checks, scarlet cap, Lady Mehta's Flashlight. Then Volteface, red with brown sleeves and black cap. Then pink and green, green cap – a small man, even smaller than the others – Ted Mullins, famous with Dark Invader.

Quarterback, Backgammon, Volteface, Dark Invader, Flashlight. That made five but there were eleven runners; six more to come: Racing Demon, Postillion, Bezique, Tetrazone and Moonlighter. Last of all Ching, peacock jacket, white sleeves, white cap, having his first run in the Viceroy's Cup on Green-sleeves, owned by a syndicate and trained by John Quillan. At the bell they came into the paddock where the trainers were gathered while the grooms led the horses round and round.

Then came orders to mount, quick hands swung the little hard men in brilliant silks into absurd saddles. A last tug at girths and a look at stirrup leathers –

THE DARK HORSE

Streaky's powerful legs were tucked under him until he seemed almost to kneel on the horse's withers. Dark Invader – "Hell of a horse," said someone in the crowd, but the little Mullins seemed to sit him quite calmly. On the grey, Quarterback, was a solid little chunk of a man, snub nose, blue jowl – the English jockey, Tim Stubbs – Quarterback was a hell of a horse, too. Then Flashlight, little head, little short ears, bit of white in his eye – a sporting print racehorse – and his English jockey Syd Johnson on top, white as a sheet and sweating. "He has a weight problem, poor devil," – then Willie Hunt with Racing Demon.

It was time for the parade. The horses gathered at the start, walked down in single file past the stands and crowds – it seemed half Calcutta was gathered on the far side of the rails – past the finish in order of the race card, Dark Invader five behind Backgammon and Streaky. Did he hear the cries of "Darkie!" "Darkie!" that came pitched louder than ever from the crowd? Then they came back, one by one, at a fast canter with a slap of the reins, a flutter of silk and the sweet smell of horses and bruised grass.

"The one race I should really like to watch," said Mother Morag, "is this one. I, who thought I should never want to watch a race again." Dahlia felt the same. It was not only the dress she had seen at Hall and Anderson's, silk in her favourite apricot with lace and the sweetest sunshade with a tassel, it was Ted and Dark Invader. "If we all could have gone, the children too." The bandar-log had, of course, gone down to the races with the spare syces who put them up on their shoulders, but Dahlia knew she had to stay at home.

Back at the start the stream of orders came from the Starter who had horses facing the wrong way, breaking out, sidling round. There was swearing, cries of, "No, sir. No," all plainly heard in the stands. Mr. Leventine, sweating under the hat he had exchanged for his topee, mopped his forehead; his rosy face was growing purple. John's was white. Never had Ted looked so small, hunched and old; Dark Invader never as big and as intimidating. Yet John noticed Ted's easy seat, the quiet rein, the horse's ears pricked. Dark Invader was eager. Eager! thought John, marvelling.

The gate went up. The Timekeeper pressed the button on the watch before the sharp bang of the rising barrier had time to reach him. The next moment the field surged past with thunder of hooves, shouts, a half-frightened curse as they raced for position on the first bend. In a matter of seconds the mass of manes, nostrils, faces half-glimpsed, resolved itself into a procession of strong quarters with the little taut white bottoms of the jockeys atop bobbing away into the distance.

"They're all there," said the Assistant Judge who had checked that nothing had been left at the post.

The Senior Judge began to read the race to the other judges. "Volteface leads, followed by Quarterback. Racing Demon and Dark Invader moving up on the rails."

The field strung out along the back stretch, coloured beads sliding along above the whiteness of the distant rail, the white domes of the Victoria Memorial behind them. The Senior Judge's voice, measured and calm, went on: "Racing Demon, Postillion, Quarterback, Backgammon, Volteface, Dark Invader, Bezique, Flashlight, Tetrazone, Moonlighter and Greensleeves." Then, "Same order. Moonlighter and Greensleeves tailing off."

They were racing now three furlongs out, going faster, fighting for position, and then it happened. John, watching through his binoculars, drew a quick breath. On the Calcutta racecourse, the final bend is sharp before the short run in. "But I had seen," Ted told him afterwards. "Seen what them bunch had cooked up. All of them got together to look after me. Streaky, Joe, Syd Johnson, Tim, the lot – 'cept Willie. They knew it, that bend, and what they done was, they draws together to block it. All five of them. Strewth! For a flash I thought I'd have to pull the Invader but he . . . as if I'd told him, he followed our pattern."

"Our pattern?"

"What you told me first time, sir – go for the outer rail, only he did it hisself!" John saw something dark swing clear of the mass of horses to take a line of its own, exactly on that outer rail. "Yes, went round the outside and, s'help me God, if he wasn't so damn good they couldn't catch us," said Ted.

The main body of the race came thundering down the straight as the Judge's voice rose in excitement. "Backgammon, Volteface, Racing Demon," and, to the Timekeeper, "Get Backgammon's number ready," but the dark horse on the outside was gaining ground and growing larger with every stride, bright colours, pink and green, pink and green, and the cries of "Darkie!" "Darkie!" grew to a roar. The calm voice never faltered. "Now it's Dark Invader, Backgammon, Volteface – get Dark Invader's number ready and hold it – Dark Invader, Backgammon, Racing Demon, Volteface." Then, in ringing tones of command, "One, Dark Invader, Two, Racing Demon, Three, Backgammon. Four and Five, Volteface and Postillion. Two lengths, half length, short head, short head. Right. Time?" he asked the Timekeeper. "Three minutes, four and three quarter seconds. Agreed? Right. Dark Invader."

"Dark Invader," and, with a rattle and squeak of unoiled pulleys, an attendant hoisted aloft the numbers of the first, second, third and fourth horses in the Viceroy's Cup.

Mr. Leventine gave a dinner at Firpo's for forty people. His guests included Sir Readymoney and Lady Mehta, the Commissioner of Police, Bunny and Captain Mack who both left early 'for another engagement'. John Quillan and Dahlia were asked but did not go. Sir Humphrey proposed the toast.

It was a banquet of eight courses in the Edwardian style, with hors d'oeuvres followed by turtle soup: then the local crayfish doing duty for lobsters and echoing Mr. Leventine's racing colours on a bed of green salad. Then quails, stuffed, on saddle-shaped pieces of toast and a guinea-fowl with almond sauce.

There was a needed pause for a sorbet, coloured

appropriately pink and green, accompanied by brown Russian cigarettes before, with new energy, the diners attacked a saddle of lamb. Then came a gateau with a portrait of Dark Invader in chocolate icing and an enormous replica of the Viceroy's Cup in golden foil which, cut open, revealed an ice pudding.

They finished with devils on horseback – bacon wrapped around a prune. "Don't you think they'll have had enough without that?" asked John.

"But it's so suitable," wailed Mr. Leventine and included it. The wines, beginning with dry sherry for the hors d'oeuvres, ran through Chablis, a Rudesheimer 1929, claret, Château Cheval Blanc, to champagne, Veuve Clicquot, ending with Madeira and brandy.

There was a band and a cabaret.

Ted gave a supper party on his verandah for the bandar-log. John and Dahlia were invited and came. The menu was sausages and ice-cream; for John and Dahlia there was whisky and champagne but, when Dark Invader was led round by Sadiq and Ali for the toast, it was drunk in sherbert by the children, Sadiq, Ali and Ted. The entertainment was fireworks which Bunny and Captain Mack were in time to help let off.

No-one seeing Mr. Leventine rise in all the glory of his evening tails, white tie, diamond dress studs, his florid yet innocent happiness, could have suspected he had spent the evening in a battle – a battle with himself.

He had led in his winner to tumultuous applause and an uproar from the crowd. Ted's face was screwed

195

into a hundred delighted wrinkles. Dark Invader lopped his ears, inclined his head and looked calm and unembarrassed.

Later in the afternoon Mr. Leventine was graciously given the golden Cup by the Viceroy and made an almost equally gracious speech, impeccably modest, paying tribute to John Quillan and Ted and Dark Invader himself.

Then he had made his announcement. Dark Invader, he said, would probably race again next winter, so 'look out', but he would then be retired and sent to stud, but not in England; here Mr. Leventine gathered himself to his full size and extended his hand to Lady Mehta who was standing by him. The Stud would be here in India for the encouragement of Indian breeding and racing. A Stud newly built and run on model lines, a venture made possible by the co-operation of his, Mr. Leventine's, dear friends, Sir Prakash and Lady Mehta and – he extended the other hand to Bunny – His Highness the Maharajah of Malwa. The applause was tremendous, but Mr. Leventine held up his hand for silence. "You will be glad to hear that with Dark Invader goes his inseparable other half, his jockey Ted Mullins, who will be our head stud-groom. No-one," said Mr. Leventine, "can think of one without the other."

No speech could have been more welcome, none more heartily endorsed. Mr. Leventine would be in the company now of people, "*People*," he said reverently, and it was sure that he would be a Steward now.

When he left the racecourse, he had gone straight to

the stables to see Dark Invader comfortably bedded down and warmly rugged; the Cup meant nothing to him except that he was tired. He only raised his head hoping for a tidbit – he still had a hankering for bread and salt – but Mr. Leventine gave him the Kulu apples that had shocked Sister Ignatius, and large pieces of sugar-cane. There was a bonus of a hundred rupees for Sadiq, fifty for Ali – then Mr. Leventine went to the annex to confirm his present to Ted.

"I hope you are pleased. I should have asked you before I made that announcement," but Ted had heard no announcement; he had been too overcome and too full of pride in Dark Invader to listen to any speech, "except they all went on and on, it seemed to me, and I never heard such clapping." Now, "A stud!" he said when Mr. Leventine had explained and John endorsed it. Both John and Bunny were with Ted. "You . . . you, sir, are going to have a stud farm?"

"Indeed yes." Mr. Leventine waved his – now, to Ted, magic – hand. "Land has been bought, building commenced. It will be a model, financed by me, Sir Prakash and Lady Mehta and . . . and," he was not quite sure what title to give Bunny – Highness or just Maharajah. "And. . ."

"And me," said Bunny. "Yes, the P.P. are letting me put money in. They actually believe one of my ideas is sound – even my old Eminence does."

"And if we succeed," said Mr. Leventine, "Mr. Quillan may join us. It will not be a paltry stud."

"And you want me . . . as head groom?" Ted could hardly say it.

"Who else?" Mr. Leventine had reverted to his 'who'. "Don't forget who will be the first to stand at stud – Dark Invader."

Ted had a sudden vision. Green grass and white-railed paddocks. Dark Invader, a portly, heavy-crested patriarch, and he, Ted, his companion to the end of his days. The whole, in the true tradition of visions and memories of childhood, suffused with golden sunlight. "Gor blimey!" and, for once, Ted said aloud, "If only Ella could know."

When Mr. Leventine left to go home and dress for his banquet, the brief Calcutta twilight had come and gone; lights were twinkling across the Maidan with smaller pinpricks from the beggar camp-fires. This time of dusk always made him feel a little sad and lonely, as if something were lacking in his busy successful life, but not tonight, thought Mr. Leventine. Surely not tonight, but, even half an hour later, dressed and standing as he liked to do in front of his library mantelpiece, it persisted. Dark Invader's cups were safely rearranged, there had been no need for that moment of panic; three cups were on the left, the goblet, quaich and rosebowl on the right and, in the centre, the golden Cup on its slender graceful stem – the Viceroy had been generous. Tomorrow it would be taken to be engraved, but now the library lamps caught the gold, sending soft rays into Mr. Leventine's eyes. The Cup would go with him to the banquet where it would be put on a stand; he had thought of filling it with champagne and passing it round, "like a loving cup", he had told John – 'loving cup' had sounded beautiful to Mr. Leventine – but John had said he thought it might be ostentatious, another new word.

In all Mr. Leventine's life there had never been a more happy and successful day; then why should this annoying thought come up that something more was needed to complete it? That something was lacking? "Nonsense, nonsense," Mr. Leventine told himself. "This is needless," and again as when, like his mother, he was being severe, he said aloud, "Casimir Alaric Bruce, this is non-sense," but, though he repeated that here, in his own opulent library, the feeling persisted. Worse, he knew what it was as surely as if another voice had told him! "The Stake money." "But it's mine – I earned it!" argued Mr. Leventine. "Wasn't it I who had the acumen, the courage?" Undoubtedly, "and I need it", but that truly was nonsense. That very morning Mr. Leventine had rounded off an extremely cosy deal with Valparaiso – cosy was his word for the swelling of his already swollen bank account.

How the thought about the Stake money had come to him he did not know; perhaps it was those mean little beggar fires; perhaps because, passing the Convent, he had thought of Mother Morag and the Sisters, and had wondered if they were warm enough. He was almost sure not. "But what is that to do with me?" he asked himself. "Look what they have extorted from me already."

"Not exactly extorted," said this other inexorable voice, and he could hear again what Mother Morag had told him: "Of course we would have given you Dark Invader back in the end. We just wanted to see if you were generous."

"And wasn't it generous? That horse cost a thousand rupees, a thousand for a country-bred! – and I would have given the buggy as well. Is it my fault they refused it?" But the refusal had stayed in his mind. "We couldn't have that expensive buggy. We are Sisters of Poverty, *poverty*, Mr. Leventine. The poor don't have buggies, though they might have a cart for work." He winced as he remembered his drive in the cart. "Well, I have given a new cart. Enough – enough!" said Mr. Leventine and he clapped his hands – there were no bells in Mr. Leventine's flat; a servant, immaculate in white clothes with a golden cummerband and gold band in his turban, was always at hand to answer that clap, and, "Bring me a large whisky and soda," said Mr. Leventine and lit a cigar.

The whisky made him more comfortable. The Stake money had certainly been earned. "Look what I have spent on that horse," but, "Not very much," the voice might now have been John Quillan's. "You got him as a bargain. You said that yourself and, as it turned out, you got Ted Mullins too."

"Well, I have not been mean. I have given lavish presents."

"Were you trying to buy goodwill?" That was a hard thought and Mr. Leventine blinked almost as if tears had come into his eyes, and it was not entirely true. He had enjoyed choosing those presents, particularly the air-guns – he was sad about the air-guns – and in thinking about the people the presents were for, particularly Ted's saddle, he had felt enormous pleasure; still more in telling Ted about the Stud, in seeing a gleam of real hope and enthusiasm in John Quillan's eyes and in hearing Dahlia's ecstatic, "Oh John! It would be so wonderful for the children." It made him, Mr. Leventine, feel like a magician, the sort of feeling he had had when the old Sister had said, "Bless you," but, "It's an infernal nuisance being a blessing," said Mr. Leventine, "and so expensive."

"Sahib – it is almost eight o'clock. Car is waiting. Time to go." Relief filled Mr. Leventine and he threw his cigar in the mock grate. His head bearer was holding his coat and white silk scarf, and the butler went to lift down reverently the golden Cup and its stand which he would take to the banquet. The Viceroy's Cup, but the Stake money. . . .

Mr. Leventine saw the menu which had been propped beside the Cup, a gold embellished card with pictures of little horses:

VINS	MENU
Fino San Patricio	Hors d'oeuvres Variés
	POTAGE
Chablis	Tortue Clair
	POISSON
Rudesheimer 1929	Langoustines Mayonnaise Salade Verte
	ENTREES
Château Cheval Blanc 1928	Cailles farcies à cheval

His eyes strayed from the menu back to the golden Cup. "Have you ever been hungry, Mr. Leventine?" It was the voice of the Chief Commissioner whom he would meet in a few minutes.

"Hell fire and damnation," cried Mr. Leventine and, to the servants, "Wait," and he went to his huge writing desk and took out a cheque book.

"Do you see what I see?" asked Mother Morag.

She passed her hand over her eyes, then looked again, "Do you read what I read?" she asked Sister Ignatius.

Sister Ignatius read and had to sit down suddenly.

After a stunned silence Mother Morag whispered, "Fifty thousand rupees!" and, presently, "We can pay off the mortgage on the new infirmary," she said.

"Perhaps we could install fans."

"Open that new kitchen."

Next day, Sister Ignatius, who was not given to such things, cut out a newspaper photograph of Dark Invader and framed it in passe-partout. Mother Morag allowed her to hang it in the Chapel.

Epilogue

It was two years later. A telegram came to Mr. Leventine, a duplicate to John Quillan, from Bangalore. It read, "Fairytale's colt born just after midnight. All well," and Ted, in his enthusiasm, had added, "Strikingly handsome. Dead ringer for Dark Invader," "Which means," Captain Mack explained to Mr. Leventine, "that it's Dark Invader all over again."

"How does Ted know?" asked John. "He wasn't there when Dark Invader was born."

"Here's hoping," said Mr. Leventine. "Our first foal."

"By Dark Invader out of Fairytale," Captain Mack said thoughtfully. "I think you should call him Dark Legend."